The Short Stories of F. Anstey

Volume I

F. Anstey was the pseudonym of Thomas Anstey Guthrie who was born in Kensington, London on August 8th, 1856, to Augusta Amherst Austen, an organist and composer, and Thomas Anstey Guthrie., a prosperous military tailor

Anstey was educated at King's College School and then at Trinity Hall, Cambridge. Although his education was first rate Anstey could only manage a third-class degree; A Gentlemen's degree as it was euphemistically known.

In 1880 he was called to the bar. However this career path rapidly fell away in his desire to become an author. The successful publication of Vice Versa, in 1882, with the premise of a substitution of a father for his schoolboy son, made his name and reputation as a refreshing and original humorist.

The following year he published a rather more serious work, The Giant's Robe. Interestingly the story is about a plagiarist and Anstey was, ironically, accused of plagiarism in writing the work. Despite good reviews both he and his public knew that his writing career was to be that of a humorist.

In the following years he published prolifically beginning with; The Black Poodle (1884), The Tinted Venus (1885), A Fallen Idol (1886), and Baboo Jabberjee B.A. (1897).

Anstey worked not only as a novelist and short story writer but was also a valued member of the staff at the humorous Punch magazine, in which his voces populi and his parodies of a reciter's stock-piece (Burglar Bill) represent perhaps his best work.

In 1901, his successful farce, The Man from Blankleys, based on a story that originally appeared in Punch, was first produced on stage at the Prince of Wales Theatre, in London.

Anstey had become a writer, and a successful one at that, of many talents.

Many more of his stories were made into plays and films over the years. Others were simply taken for the premise alone, usually with no credit to the original author.

By the end of the First World War Anstey's original publications had slowed to a crawl and he seemed rather more interested in translating and publishing some works of Moliere.

Thomas Anstey Guthrie died of pneumonia on March 10th, 1934 in London.

His self-deprecating autobiography, A Long Retrospect, was published in 1936.

Index of Contents

A Canine Ishmael

(FROM THE NOTES OF A DINER-OUT)

'Tell me,' she said suddenly, with a pretty imperiousness that seemed to belong to her, 'are you fond of dogs?' How we arrived at the subject I forget now, but I know she had just been describing how a collie at a dog-show she had visited lately had suddenly thrown his forepaws round her neck in a burst of affection—a proceeding which, in my own mind (although I prudently kept this to myself), I considered less astonishing than she appeared to do.

For I had had the privilege of taking her in to dinner, and the meal had not reached a very advanced stage before I had come to the conclusion that she was the most charming, if not the loveliest, person I had ever met.

It was fortunate for me that I was honestly able to answer her question in a satisfactory manner, for, had it been otherwise, I doubt whether she would have deigned to bestow much more of her conversation upon me.

'Then I wonder,' she said next, meditatively, 'if you would care to hear about a dog that belonged to—to someone I know very well? Or would it bore you?'

I am very certain that if she had volunteered to relate the adventures of Telemachus, or the history of the Thirty Years' War, I should have accepted the proposal with a quite genuine gratitude. As it was, I made it sufficiently plain that I should care very much indeed to hear about that dog.

She paused for a moment to reject an unfortunate entree (which I confess to doing my best to console), and then she began her story. I shall try to set it down as nearly as possible in her own words, although I cannot hope to convey the peculiar charm and interest that she gave it for me. It was not, I need hardly say, told all at once, but was subject to the inevitable interruptions which render a dinner-table intimacy so piquantly precarious.

'This dog,' she began quietly, without any air of beginning a story, 'this dog was called Pepper. He was not much to look at—rather a rough, mongrelly kind of animal; and he and a young man had kept house together for a long time, for the young man was a bachelor and lived in chambers by himself. He always used to say that he didn't like to get engaged to anyone, because he was sure it would put Pepper out so fearfully. However, he met somebody at last who made him forget about Pepper, and he proposed and was accepted—and then, you know,' she added, as a little dimple came in her cheek, 'he had to go home and break the news to the dog.'

She had just got to this point, when, taking advantage of a pause she made, the man on her other side (who was, I daresay, strictly within his rights, although I remember at the time considering him a pushing beast) struck in with some remark which she turned to answer, leaving me leisure to reflect.

I was feeling vaguely uncomfortable about this story; something, it would be hard to say what, in her way of mentioning Pepper's owner made me suspect that he was more than a mere acquaintance of hers.

Was it she, then, who was responsible for—? It was no business of mine, of course; I had never met her in my life till that evening—but I began to be impatient to hear the rest.

And at last she turned to me again: 'I hope you haven't forgotten that I was in the middle of a story. You haven't? And you would really like me to go on? Well, then—oh yes, when Pepper was told, he was naturally a little annoyed at first. I daresay he considered he ought to have been consulted previously. But, as soon as he had seen the lady, he withdrew all opposition—which his master declared was a tremendous load off his mind, for Pepper was rather a difficult dog, and slow as a rule to take strangers into his affections, a little snappy and surly, and very easily hurt or offended. Don't you know dogs who are sensitive like that? I do, and I'm always so sorry for them—they feel little things so much, and one never can find out what's the matter, and have it out with them! Sometimes it's shyness; once I had a dog who was quite painfully shy—self-consciousness it was really, I suppose, for he always fancied everybody was looking at him, and often when people were calling he would come and hide his face in the folds of my dress till they had gone—it was too ridiculous! But about Pepper. He was devoted to his new mistress from the very first. I am not sure that she was quite so struck with him, for he was not at all a lady's dog, and his manners had been very much neglected. Still, she came quite to like him in time; and when they were married, Pepper went with them for the honeymoon.'

'When they were married!' I glanced at the card which lay half-hidden by her plate. Surely Miss So-and-so was written on it?—yes, it was certainly 'Miss.' It was odd that such a circumstance should have increased my enjoyment of the story, perhaps—but it undoubtedly did.

'After the honeymoon,' my neighbour continued, 'they came to live in the new house, which was quite a tiny one, and Pepper was a very important personage in it indeed. He had his mistress all to himself for the greater part of most days, as his master had to be away in town; so she used to talk to him intimately, and tell him more than she would have thought of confiding to most people. Sometimes, when she thought there was no fear of callers coming, she would make him play, and this was quite a new sensation for Pepper, who was a serious-minded animal, and took very solemn views of life. At first he hadn't the faintest idea what was expected of him; it must have been rather like trying to romp with a parish beadle, he was so intensely respectable! But as soon as he once grasped the notion and understood that no liberty was intended, he lent himself to it readily enough and learnt to gambol quite creditably. Then he was made much of in all sorts of ways; she washed him twice a week with her very own hands—which his master would never have dreamt of doing—and she was always trying new ribbons on his complexion. That rather bored him at first, but it ended by making him a little conceited about his appearance. Altogether he was dearly fond of her, and I don't believe he had ever been happier in all his life than he was in those days. Only, unfortunately, it was all too good to last.'

Here I had to pass olives or something to somebody, and the other man, seeing his chance, and, to do him justice, with no idea that he was interrupting a story, struck in once more, so that the history of Pepper had to remain in abeyance for several minutes.

My uneasiness returned. Could there be a mistake about that name-card after all? Cards do get re-arranged sometimes, and she seemed to know that young couple so very intimately. I tried to remember whether I had been introduced to her as a Miss or Mrs. So-and-so, but without success. There is some fatality which generally distracts one's attention at the critical moment of introduction, and in this case it was perhaps easily accounted for. My turn came again, and she took up her tale once more. 'I think when I left off I was saying that Pepper's happiness was too good to last. And so it was. For his mistress was ill, and, though he snuffed and scratched and whined at the door of her room for ever so long, they wouldn't let him in. But he managed to slip in one day somehow, and jumped up on her lap and licked her hands and face, and almost went out of his mind with joy at seeing her again. Only (I told you he was a sensitive dog) it gradually struck him that she was not quite so pleased to see him as usual—and presently he found out the reason. There was another animal there, a new pet, which seemed to take up a good deal of her attention. Of course you guess what that was—but Pepper had never seen a baby before, and he took it as a personal slight and was dreadfully offended. He simply walked straight out of the room and downstairs to the kitchen, where he stayed for days.

'I don't think he enjoyed his sulk much, poor doggie; perhaps he had an idea that when they saw how much he took it to heart they would send the baby away. But as time went on and this didn't seem to occur to them, he decided to come out of the sulks and look over the matter, and he came back quite prepared to resume the old footing. Only everything was different. No one seemed to notice that he was in the room now, and his mistress never invited him to have a game; she even forgot to have him washed—and one of his peculiarities was that he had no objection to soap and warm water. The worst of it was, too, that before very long the baby followed him into the sitting-room, and, do what he could, he couldn't make the stupid little thing understand that it had no business there. If you think of it, a baby must strike a dog as a very inferior little animal: it can't bark (well, yes, it can howl), but it's no good whatever with rats, and yet everybody makes a tremendous fuss about it! The baby got all poor Pepper's bows now; and his mistress played games with it, though Pepper felt he could have done it ever so much better, but he was never allowed to join in. So he used to lie on a rug and pretend he didn't mind, though, really, I'm certain he felt it horribly. I always believe, you know, that people never give dogs half credit enough for feeling things, don't you?

'Well, at last came the worst indignity of all: Pepper was driven from his rug—his own particular rug—to make room for the baby; and when he had got away into a corner to cry quietly, all by himself, that wretched baby came and crawled after him and pulled his tail!

'He always had been particular about his tail, and never allowed anybody to touch it but very intimate friends, and even then under protest, so you can imagine how insulted he felt.

'It was too much for him, and he lost the last scrap of temper he had. They said he bit the baby, and I'm afraid he did—though not enough really to hurt it; still, it howled fearfully, of course, and from that moment it was all over with poor Pepper—he was a ruined dog!

'When his master came home that evening he was told the whole story. Pepper's mistress said she would be ever so sorry to part with him, but, after his misbehaviour, she should never know a moment's peace until he was out of the house—it really wasn't safe for baby!

'And his master was sorry, naturally; but I suppose he was beginning rather to like the baby himself, and so the end of it was that Pepper had to go. They did all they could for him; found him a comfortable home, with a friend who was looking out for a good house-dog, and wasn't particular about breed, and, after that, they heard nothing of him for a long while. And, when they did hear, it was rather a bad report: the friend could do nothing with Pepper at all; he had to tie him up in the stable, and then he snapped at everyone who came near, and howled all night—they were really almost afraid of him.

'So when Pepper's mistress heard that, she felt more thankful than ever that the dog had been sent away, and tried to think no more about him. She had quite forgotten all about it, when, one day, a new nursemaid, who had taken the baby out for an airing, came back with a terrible account of a savage dog which had attacked them, and leaped up at the perambulator so persistently that it was as much as she could do to drive it away. And even then Pepper's mistress did not associate the dog with him; she thought he had been destroyed long ago.

'But the next time the nurse went out with the baby she took a thick stick with her, in case the dog should come again. And no sooner had she lifted the perambulator over the step, than the dog did come again, exactly as if he had been lying in wait for them ever since outside the gate.

'The nurse was a strong country girl, with plenty of pluck, and as the dog came leaping and barking about in a very alarming way, she hit him as hard as she could on his head. The wonder is she did not kill him on the spot, and, as it was, the blow turned him perfectly giddy and silly for a time, and he ran round and round in a dazed sort of way—do you think you could lower that candle-shade just a little? Thanks!' she broke off suddenly, as I obeyed. 'Well, she was going to strike again, when her mistress rushed out, just in time to stop her. For, you see, she had been watching at the window, and although the poor beast was miserably thin, and rough, and neglected-looking, she knew at once that it must be Pepper, and that he was not in the least mad or dangerous, but only trying his best to make his peace with the baby. Very likely his dignity or his conscience or something wouldn't let him come back quite at once, you know; and perhaps he thought he had better get the baby on his side first. And then all at once, his mistress—I heard all this through her, of course—his mistress suddenly remembered how devoted Pepper had been to her, and how fond she had once been of him, and when she saw him standing, stupid and shivering, there, her heart softened to him, and she went to make it up with him, and tell him that he was forgiven and should come back and be her dog again, just as in the old days!—'

Here she broke off for a moment. I did not venture to look at her, but I thought her voice trembled a little when she spoke again. 'I don't quite know why I tell you all this. There was a time when I never could bear the end of it myself,' she said; 'but I have begun, and I will finish now. Well, Pepper's mistress went towards him, and called him; but—whether he was still too dizzy to quite understand who she was, or whether his pride came uppermost again, poor dear! I don't know—but he gave her just one look (she says she will never forget it—never; it went straight to her heart), and then he walked very slowly and deliberately away.

'She couldn't bear it; she followed; she felt she simply must make him understand how very, very sorry she was for him; but the moment he heard her he began to run faster and faster, until he was out of reach and out of sight, and she had to come back. I know she was crying bitterly by that time.'

'And he never came back again?' I asked, after a silence.

'Never again!' she said softly; 'that was the very last they ever saw or heard of him. And—and I've always loved every dog since for Pepper's sake!'

'I'm almost glad he did decline to come back,' I declared; 'it served his mistress right—she didn't deserve anything else!'

'Ah, I didn't want you to say that!' she protested; 'she never meant to be so unkind—it was all for the baby's sake!'

I was distinctly astonished, for all her sympathy in telling the story had seemed to lie in the other direction.

'You don't mean to say,' I cried involuntarily, 'that you can find any excuses for her? I did not expect you would take the baby's part!'

'But I did,' she confessed, with lowered eyes—'I did take the baby's part—it was all my doing that Pepper was sent away—I have been sorry enough for it since!'

It was her own story she had been telling at second-hand after all—and she was not Miss So-and-so! I had entirely forgotten the existence of any other members of the party but our two selves, but at the moment of this discovery—which was doubly painful—I was recalled by a general rustle to the fact that we were at a dinner-party, and that our hostess had just given the signal.

As I rose and drew back my chair to allow my neighbour to pass, she raised her eyes for a moment and said almost meekly:

'I was the baby, you see!'

The Curse of the Catafalques

I.

Unless I am very much mistaken, until the time when I was subjected to the strange and exceptional experience which I now propose to relate, I had never been brought into close contact with anything of a supernatural description. At least if I ever was, the circumstance can have made no lasting impression upon me, as I am quite unable to recall it. But in the 'Curse of the Catafalques' I was confronted with a horror so weird and so altogether unusual, that I doubt whether I shall ever succeed in wholly forgetting it—and I know that I have never felt really well since.

It is difficult for me to tell my story intelligibly without some account of my previous history by way of introduction, although I will to make it as little diffuse as I may.

I had not been a success at home; I was an orphan, and, in my anxiety to please a wealthy uncle upon whom I was practically dependent, I had consented to submit myself to a series of competitive examinations for quite a variety of professions, but in each successive instance I achieved the same disheartening failure. Some explanation of this may, no doubt, be found in the fact that, with a fatal want of forethought, I had entirely omitted to prepare myself by any particular course of study—which, as I discovered too late, is almost indispensable to success in these intellectual contests.

My uncle himself took this view, and conceiving—not without discernment—that I was by no means likely to retrieve myself by any severe degree of application in the future, he had me shipped out to Australia, where he had correspondents and friends who would put things in my way.

They did put several things in my way—and, as might have been expected, I came to grief over every one of them, until at length, having given a fair trial to each opening that had been provided for me, I began to perceive that my uncle had made a grave mistake in believing me suited for a colonial career.

I resolved to return home and convince him of his error, and give him one more opportunity of repairing it; he had failed to discover the best means of utilising my undoubted ability, yet I would not reproach him (nor do I reproach him even now), for I too have felt the difficulty.

In pursuance of my resolution, I booked my passage home by one of the Orient liners from Melbourne to London. About an hour before the ship was to leave her moorings, I went on board and made my way at once to the state-room which I was to share with a fellow passenger, whose acquaintance I then made for the first time.

He was a tall cadaverous young man of about my own age, and my first view of him was not encouraging, for when I came in, I found him rolling restlessly on the cabin floor, and uttering hollow groans.

'This will never do,' I said, after I had introduced myself; 'if you're like this now, my good sir, what will you be when we're fairly out at sea? You must husband your resources for that. And why trouble to roll? The ship will do all that for you, if you will only have patience.'

He explained, somewhat brusquely, that he was suffering from mental agony, not sea-sickness; and by a little pertinacious questioning (for I would not allow myself to be rebuffed) I was soon in possession of the secret which was troubling my companion, whose name, as I also learned, was Augustus McFadden.

It seemed that his parents had emigrated before his birth, and he had lived all his life in the Colony, where he was contented and fairly prosperous—when an eccentric old aunt of his over in England happened to die.

She left McFadden himself nothing, having given by her will the bulk of her property to the only daughter of a baronet of ancient family, in whom she took a strong interest. But the will was not without its effect upon her existence, for it expressly mentioned the desire of the testatrix that the baronet should receive her nephew Augustus if he presented himself within a certain time, and should afford him every facility for proving his fitness for acceptance as a suitor. The alliance was merely recommended, however, not enjoined, and the gift was unfettered by any conditions.

'I heard of it first,' said McFadden, 'from Chlorine's father (Chlorine is her name, you know). Sir Paul Catafalque wrote to me, informing me of the mention of my name in my aunt's will, enclosing his daughter's photograph, and formally inviting me to come over and do my best, if my affections were not pre-engaged, to carry out the last wishes of the departed. He added that I might expect to receive shortly a packet from my aunt's executors which would explain matters fully, and in which I should find certain directions for my guidance. The photograph decided me; it was so eminently pleasing that I felt at once that my poor aunt's wishes must be sacred to me. I could not wait for the packet to arrive, and so I wrote at once to Sir Paul accepting the invitation. Yes,' he added, with another of the hollow groans, 'miserable wretch that I am, I pledged my honour to present myself as a suitor, and now—now—here I am, actually embarked upon the desperate errand!'

He seemed inclined to begin to roll again here, but I stopped him. 'Really,' I said, 'I think in your place, with an excellent chance—for I presume the lady's heart is also disengaged—with an excellent chance of winning a baronet's daughter with a considerable fortune and a pleasing appearance, I should bear up better.'

'You think so,' he rejoined,'but you do not know all! The very day after I had despatched my fatal letter, my aunt's explanatory packet arrived. I tell you that when I read the hideous revelations it contained, and knew to what horrors I had innocently pledged myself, my hair stood on end, and I believe it has remained on end ever since. But it was too late. Here I am, engaged to carry out a task from which my inmost soul recoils. Ah, if I dared but retract!'

'Then why in the name of common sense, don't you retract?' I asked. 'Write and say that you much regret that a previous engagement, which you had unfortunately overlooked, deprives you of the pleasure of accepting.'

'Impossible,' he said; 'it would be agony to me to feel that I had incurred Chlorine's contempt, even though I only know her through a photograph at present. If I were to back out of it now, she would have reason to despise me, would she not?'

'Perhaps she would,' I said.

'You see my dilemma—I cannot retract; on the other hand, I dare not go on. The only thing, as I have thought lately, which could save me and my honour at the same time would be my death on the voyage out, for then my cowardice would remain undiscovered.'

'Well,' I said, 'you can die on the voyage out if you want to—there need be no difficulty about that. All you have to do is just to slip over the side some dark night when no one is looking. I tell you what,' I added (for somehow I began to feel a friendly interest in this poor slack-baked creature): 'if you don't find your nerves equal to it when it comes to the point, I don't mind giving you a leg over myself.'

'I never intended to go as far as that,' he said, rather pettishly, and without any sign of gratitude for my offer; 'I don't care about actually dying, if she could only be made to believe I had died that would be quite enough for me. I could live on here, happy in the thought that I was saved from her scorn. But how can she be made to believe it?—that's the point.'

'Precisely,' I said. 'You can hardly write yourself and inform her that you died on the voyage. You might do this, though: sail to England as you propose, and go to see her under another name, and break the sad intelligence to her.'

'Why, to be sure, I might do that!' he said, with some animation; 'I should certainly not be recognised— she can have no photograph of me, for I have never been photographed. And yet—no,' he added, with a shudder, 'it is useless. I can't do it; I dare not trust myself under that roof! I must find some other way. You have given me an idea. Listen,' he said, after a short pause: 'you seem to take an interest in me; you are going to London; the Catafalques live there, or near it, at some place called Parson's Green. Can I ask a great favour of you—would you very much mind seeking them out yourself as a fellow-voyager of mine? I could not expect you to tell a positive untruth on my account—but if, in the course of an interview with Chlorine, you could contrive to convey the impression that I died on my way to her side, you would be doing me a service I can never repay!'

'I should very much prefer to do you a service that you could repay,' was my very natural rejoinder.

'She will not require strict proof,' he continued eagerly; 'I could give you enough papers and things to convince her that you come from me. Say you will do me this kindness!'

I hesitated for some time longer, not so much, perhaps, from scruples of a conscientious kind as from a disinclination to undertake a troublesome commission for an entire stranger—gratuitously. But McFadden pressed me hard, and at length he made an appeal to springs in my nature which are never touched in vain, and I yielded.

When we had settled the question in its financial aspect, I said to McFadden, 'The only thing now is— how would you prefer to pass away? Shall I make you fall over and be devoured by a shark? That would be a picturesque end—and I could do myself justice over the shark? I should make the young lady weep considerably.'

'That won't do at all!' he said irritably; 'I can see from her face that Chlorine is a girl of a delicate sensibility, and would be disgusted by the idea of any suitor of hers spending his last cohesive moments inside such a beastly repulsive thing as a shark. I don't want to be associated in her mind with anything so unpleasant. No, sir; I will die—if you will oblige me by remembering it—of a low fever, of a non-infectious type, at sunset, gazing at her portrait with my fading eyesight and gasping her name with my last breath. She will cry more over that!'

'I might work it up into something effective, certainly,' I admitted; 'and, by the way, if you are going to expire in my state-room, I ought to know a little more about you than I do. There is time still before the tender goes; you might do worse than spend it in coaching me in your life's history.'

He gave me a few leading facts, and supplied me with several documents for study on the voyage; he even abandoned to me the whole of his travelling arrangements, which proved far more complete and serviceable than my own.

And then the 'All-ashore' bell rang, and McFadden, as he bade me farewell, took from his pocket a bulky packet. 'You have saved me,' he said. 'Now I can banish every recollection of this miserable episode. I need no longer preserve my poor aunt's directions; let them go, then.'

Before I could say anything, he had fastened something heavy to the parcel and dropped it through the cabin-light into the sea, after which he went ashore, and I have never seen nor heard of him since.

During the voyage I had leisure to think seriously over the affair, and the more I thought of the task I had undertaken, the less I liked it.

No man with the instincts of a gentleman can feel any satisfaction at rinding himself on the way to harrow up a poor young lady's feelings by a perfectly fictitious account of the death of a poor-spirited suitor who could selfishly save his reputation at her expense.

And so strong was my feeling about this from the very first, that I doubt whether, if McFadden's terms had been a shade less liberal, I could ever have brought myself to consent.

But it struck me that, under judiciously sympathetic treatment, the lady might prove not inconsolable, and that I myself might be able to heal the wound I was about to inflict.

I found a subtle pleasure in the thought of this, for, unless McFadden had misinformed me, Chlorine's fortune was considerable, and did not depend upon any marriage she might or might not make. On the other hand, I was penniless, and it seemed to me only too likely that her parents might seek to found some objection to me on that ground.

I studied the photograph McFadden had left with me; it was that of a pensive but distinctly pretty face, with an absence of firmness in it that betrayed a plastic nature. I felt certain that if I only had the recommendation, as McFadden had, of an aunt's dying wishes, it would not take me long to effect a complete conquest.

And then, as naturally as possible, came the thought—why should not I procure myself the advantages of this recommendation? Nothing could be easier; I had merely to present myself as Augustus McFadden, who was hitherto a mere name to them; the information I already possessed as to his past life would enable me to support the character, and as it seemed that the baronet lived in great seclusion, I could easily contrive to keep out of the way of the few friends and relations I had in London until my position was secure.

What harm would this innocent deception do to anyone? McFadden, even if he ever knew, would have no right to complain—he had given up all pretentions himself and if he was merely anxious to preserve his reputation, his wishes would be more than carried out, for I flattered myself that whatever ideal Chlorine might have formed of her destined suitor, I should come much nearer to it than poor McFadden could ever have done. No, he would gain, positively gain, by my assumption. He could not have counted upon arousing more than a mild regret as it was; now he would be fondly, it might be madly, loved. By proxy, it is true, but that was far more than he deserved.

Chlorine was not injured—far from it; she would have a suitor to welcome, not weep over, and his mere surname could make no possible difference to her. And lastly, it was a distinct benefit to me, for with a new name and an excellent reputation success would be an absolute certainty. What wonder, then, that the scheme, which opened out a far more manly and honourable means of obtaining a livelihood than any I had previously contemplated, should have grown more attractively feasible each day, until I resolved at last to carry it out? Let rigid moralists blame me if they will; I have never pretended to be better than the average run of mankind (though I am certainly no worse), and no one who really knows what human nature is will reproach me very keenly for obeying what was almost an instinct. And I may say this, that if ever an unfortunate man was bitterly punished for a fraud which was harmless, if not actually pious, by a visitation of intense and protracted terror, that person was I!

II.

After arriving in England, and before presenting myself at Parson's Green in my assumed character, I took one precaution against any danger there might be of my throwing away my liberty in a fit of youthful impulsiveness. I went to Somerset House, and carefully examined the probate copy of the late Miss Petronia McFadden's last will and testament.

Nothing could have been more satisfactory; a sum of between forty and fifty thousand pounds was Chlorine's unconditionally, just as McFadden had said. I searched, but could find nothing in the will whatever to prevent her property, under the then existing state of the law, from passing under the entire control of a future husband.

After this, then, I could no longer restrain my ardour, and so, one foggy afternoon about the middle of December, I found myself driving towards the house in which I reckoned upon achieving a comfortable independence.

Parson's Green was reached at last; a small triangular open space bordered on two of its sides by mean and modern erections, but on the third by some ancient mansions, gloomy and neglected-looking indeed, but with traces on them still of their former consequence.

My cab stopped before the gloomiest of them all—a square grim house with dull and small-paned windows, flanked by two narrow and projecting wings, and built of dingy brick, faced with yellow-stone. Some old scroll-work railings, with a corroded frame in the middle for a long departed oil-lamp, separated the house from the road; inside was a semicircular patch of rank grass, and a damp gravel sweep led from the heavy gate to a square portico supported by two wasted black wooden pillars.

As I stood there, after pulling the pear-shaped bell-handle, and heard the bell tinkling and jangling fretfully within, and as I glanced up at the dull house-front looming cheerless out of the fog-laden December twilight, I felt my confidence beginning to abandon me for the first time, and I really was almost inclined to give the whole thing up and run away.

Before I could make up my mind, a mouldy and melancholy butler had come slowly down the sweep and opened the gate—and my opportunity had fled. Later I remembered how, as I walked along the gravel, a wild and wailing scream pierced the heavy silence—it seemed at once a lamentation and a warning. But as the District Railway was quite near, I did not attach any particular importance to the sound at the time.

I followed the butler through a dank and chilly hall, where an antique lamp hung glimmering feebly through its panes of dusty stained glass, up a broad carved staircase, and along some tortuous panelled passages, until at length I was ushered into a long and rather low reception room, scantily furnished with the tarnished mirrors and spindle-legged brocaded furniture of a bygone century.

A tall and meagre old man, with a long white beard, and haggard, sunken black eyes, was seated at one side of the high chimney-piece, while opposite him sat a little limp old lady with a nervous expression, and dressed in trailing black robes relieved by a little yellow lace about the head and throat. As I saw them, I recognised at once that I was in the presence of Sir Paul Catafalque and his wife.

They both rose slowly, and advanced arm-in-arm in their old-fashioned way, and met me with a stately solemnity. 'You are indeed welcome,' they said in faint hollow voices. 'We thank you for this proof of your chivalry and devotion. It cannot be but that such courage and such self-sacrifice will meet with their reward!'

And although I did not quite understand how they could have discerned, as yet, that I was chivalrous and devoted, I was too glad to have made a good impression to do anything but beg them not to mention it.

And then a slender figure, with a drooping head, a wan face, and large sad eyes, came softly down the dimly-lighted room towards me, and I and my destined bride met for the first time.

As I had expected, after she had once anxiously raised her eyes, and allowed them to rest upon me, her face was lighted up by an evident relief, as she discovered that the fulfilment of my aunt's wishes would not be so distasteful to her, personally, as it might have been.

For myself, I was upon the whole rather disappointed in her; the portrait had flattered her considerably—the real Chlorine was thinner and paler than I had been led to anticipate, while there was a settled melancholy in her manner which I felt would prevent her from being an exhilarating companion.

And I must say I prefer a touch of archness and animation in womankind, and, if I had been free to consult my own tastes, should have greatly preferred to become a member of a more cheerful family. Under the circumstances, however, I was not entitled to be too particular, and I put up with it.

From the moment of my arrival I fell easily and naturally into the position of an honoured guest, who might be expected in time to form nearer and dearer relations with the family, and certainly I was afforded every opportunity of doing so.

I made no mistakes, for the diligence with which I had got up McFadden's antecedents enabled me to give perfectly satisfactory replies to most of the few allusions or questions that were addressed to me, and I drew upon my imagination for the rest.

But those days I spent in the baronet's family were far from lively: the Catafalques went nowhere; they seemed to know nobody; at least no visitors ever called or dined there while I was with them, and the time dragged slowly on in a terrible monotony in that dim tomb of a house, which I was not expected to leave except for very brief periods, for Sir Paul would grow uneasy if I walked out alone—even to Putney.

There was something, indeed, about the attitude of both the old people towards myself which I could only consider as extremely puzzling. They would follow me about with a jealous care, blended with anxious alarm, and their faces as they looked at me wore an expression of tearful admiration, touched with something of pity, as for some youthful martyr; at times, too, they spoke of the gratitude they felt, and professed a determined hopefulness as to my ultimate success.

Now I was well aware that this is not the ordinary bearing of the parents of an heiress to a suitor who, however deserving in other respects, is both obscure and penniless, and the only way in which I could account for it was by the supposition that there was some latent defect in Chlorine's temper or constitution, which entitled the man who won her to commiseration, and which would also explain their evident anxiety to get her off their hands.

But although anything of this kind would be, of course, a drawback, I felt that forty or fifty thousand pounds would be a fair set-off—and I could not expect everything.

When the time came at which I felt that I could safely speak to Chlorine of what lay nearest my heart, I found an unforeseen difficulty in bringing her to confess that she reciprocated my passion.

She seemed to shrink unaccountably from speaking the word which gave me the right to claim her, confessing that she dreaded it not for her own sake, but for mine alone, which struck me as an unpleasantly morbid trait in so young a girl.

Again and again I protested that I was willing to run all risks—as I was—and again and again she resisted, though always more faintly, until at last my efforts were successful, and I forced from her lips the assent which was of so much importance to me.

But it cost her a great effort, and I believe she even swooned immediately afterwards; but this is only conjecture, as I lost no time in seeking Sir Paul and clenching the matter before Chlorine had time to retract.

He heard what I had to tell him with a strange light of triumph and relief in his weary eyes. 'You have made an old man very happy and hopeful,' he said. 'I ought, even now to deter you, but I am too selfish for that. And you are young and brave and ardent; why need we despair? I suppose,' he added, looking keenly at me, 'you would prefer as little delay as possible?'

'I should indeed,' I replied. I was pleased, for I had not expected to find him so sensible as that.

'Then leave all preliminaries to me; when the day and time have been settled, I will let you know. As you are aware, it will be necessary to have your signature to this document; and here, my boy, I must in conscience warn you solemnly that by signing you make your decision irrevocable—irrevocable, you understand?'

When I had heard this, I need scarcely say that I was all eagerness to sign; so great was my haste that I did not even try to decipher the somewhat crabbed and antiquated writing in which the terms of the agreement were set out.

I was anxious to impress the baronet with a sense of my gentlemanly feeling and the confidence I had in him, while I naturally presumed that, since the contract was binding upon me, the baronet would, as a man of honour, hold it equally conclusive on his own side.

As I look back upon it now, it seems simply extraordinary that I should have been so easily satisfied, have taken so little pains to find out the exact position in which I was placing myself; but, with the ingenuous confidence of youth, I fell an easy victim, as I was to realise later with terrible enlightenment.

'Say nothing of this to Chlorine,' said Sir Paul, as I handed him the document signed, 'until the final arrangements are made; it will only distress her unnecessarily.'

I wondered why at the time, but I promised to obey, supposing that he knew best, and for some days after that I made no mention to Chlorine of the approaching day which was to witness our union.

As we were continually together, I began to regard her with an esteem which I had not thought possible at first. Her looks improved considerably under the influence of happiness, and I found she could converse intelligently enough upon several topics, and did not bore me nearly as much as I was fully prepared for.

And so the time passed less heavily, until one afternoon the baronet took me aside mysteriously. 'Prepare yourself, Augustus' (they had all learned to call me Augustus), he said; 'all is arranged. The event upon which our dearest hopes depend is fixed for to-morrow—in the Grey Chamber of course, and at midnight.'

I thought this a curious time and place for the ceremony, but I had divined his eccentric passion for privacy and retirement, and only imagined that he had procured some very special form of licence.

'But you do not know the Grey Chamber,' he added. 'Come with me, and I will show you where it is.' And he led me up the broad staircase, and, stopping at the end of a passage before an immense door covered with black baize and studded with brass nails, which gave it a hideous resemblance to a gigantic coffin lid, he pressed a spring, and it fell slowly back.

I saw a long dim gallery, whose very existence nothing in the external appearance of the mansion had led me to suspect; it led to a heavy oaken door with cumbrous plates and fastenings of metal.

'To-morrow night is Christmas Eve, as you are doubtless aware,' he said in a hushed voice. 'At twelve, then, you will present yourself at yonder door—the door of the Grey Chamber—where you must fulfil the engagement you have made.'

I was surprised at his choosing such a place for the ceremony; it would have been more cheerful in the long drawing room; but it was evidently a whim of his, and I was too happy to think of opposing it. I hastened at once to Chlorine, with her father's sanction, and told her that the crowning moment of both our lives was fixed at last.

The effect of my announcement was astonishing: she fainted, for which I remonstrated with her as soon as she came to herself. 'Such extreme sensitiveness, my love,' I could not help saying, 'may be highly creditable to your sense of maidenly propriety, but allow me to say that I can scarcely regard it as a compliment.'

'Augustus,' she said, 'you must not think I doubt you; and yet—and yet—the ordeal will be a severe one for you.'

'I will steel my nerves,' I said grimly (for I was annoyed with her); 'and, after all, Chlorine, the ceremony is not invariably fatal; I have heard of the victim surviving it—occasionally.'

'How brave you are!' she said earnestly. 'I will imitate you, Augustus; I too will hope.'

I really thought her insane, which alarmed me for the validity of the marriage. 'Yes, I am weak, foolish, I know,' she continued; 'but oh, I shudder so when I think of you, away in that gloomy Grey Chamber, going through it all alone!'

This confirmed my worst fears. No wonder her parents felt grateful to me for relieving them of such a responsibility! 'May I ask where you intend to be at the time?' I inquired very quietly.

'You will not think us unfeeling,' she replied, 'but dear papa considered that such anxiety as ours would be scarcely endurable did we not seek some distraction from it; and so, as a special favour, he has procured evening orders for Sir John Soane's Museum in Lincoln's Inn Fields, where we shall drive immediately after dinner.'

I knew that the proper way to treat the insane was by reasoning with them gently, so as to place their own absurdity clearly before them. 'If you are forgetting your anxiety in Sir John Soane's Museum, while I cool my heels in the Grey Chamber,' I said, 'is it probable that any clergyman will be induced to perform the marriage ceremony? Did you really think two people can be united separately?'

She was astonished this time. 'You are joking!' she cried; 'you cannot really believe that we are to be married in—in the Grey Chamber?'

'Then will you tell me where we are to be married?' I asked. 'I think I have the right to know—it can hardly be at the Museum!'

She turned upon me with a sudden misgiving; 'I could almost fancy,' she said anxiously, 'that this is no feigned ignorance. Augustus, your aunt sent you a message—tell me, have you read it?'

Now, owing to McFadden's want of consideration, this was my one weak point—I had not read it, and thus I felt myself upon delicate ground. The message evidently related to business of importance which was to be transacted in this Grey Chamber, and as the genuine McFadden clearly knew all about it, it would have been simply suicidal to confess my own ignorance.

'Why of course, darling, of course,' I said hastily. 'You must think no more of my silly joke; there is something I have to arrange in the Grey Chamber before I can call you mine. But, tell me, why does it make you so uneasy?' I added, thinking it might be prudent to find out beforehand what formality was expected from me.

'I cannot help it—no, I cannot!' she cried, 'the test is so searching—are you sure that you are prepared at all points? I overheard my father say that no precaution could safely be neglected. I have such a terrible foreboding that, after all, this may come between us.'

It was clear enough to me now; the baronet was by no means so simple and confiding in his choice of a son-in-law as I had imagined, and had no intention, after all, of accepting me without some inquiry into my past life, my habits, and my prospects.

That he should seek to make this examination more impressive by appointing this ridiculous midnight interview for it, was only what might have been expected from an old man of his confirmed eccentricity.

But I knew I could easily contrive to satisfy the baronet, and with the idea of consoling Chlorine, I said as much. 'Why will you persist in treating me like a child, Augustus?' she broke out almost petulantly. 'They have tried to hide it all from me, but do you suppose I do not know that in the Grey Chamber you will have to encounter one far more formidable, far more difficult to satisfy, than poor dear papa?'

'I see you know more than I—more than I thought you did,' I said. 'Let us understand one another, Chlorine—tell me exactly how much you know.'

'I have told you all I know,' she said; 'it is your turn to confide in me.'

'Not even for your sweet sake, my dearest,' I was obliged to say, 'can I break the seal that is set upon my tongue. You must not press me. Come, let us talk of other things.'

But I now saw that matters were worse than I had thought; instead of the feeble old baronet I should have to deal with a stranger, some exacting and officious friend or relation perhaps, or, more probably, a keen family solicitor who would put questions I should not care about answering, and even be capable of insisting upon strict settlements.

It was that, of course; they would try to tie my hands by a strict settlement, with a brace of cautious trustees; unless I was very careful, all I should get by my marriage would be a paltry life-interest, contingent upon my surviving my wife.

This revolted me; it seems to me that when law comes in with its offensively suspicious restraints upon the husband and its indelicately premature provisions for the offspring, all the poetry of love is gone at once. By allowing the wife to receive the income 'for her separate use and free from the control of her husband,' as the phrase runs, you infallibly brush the bloom from the peach, and implant the 'little speck within the fruit' which, as Tennyson beautifully says, will widen by-and-by and make the music mute.

This may be overstrained on my part, but it represents my honest conviction; I was determined to have nothing to do with law. If it was necessary, I felt quite sure enough of Chlorine to defy Sir Paul. I would refuse to meet a family solicitor anywhere, and I intended to say so plainly at the first convenient opportunity.

III.

The opportunity came after dinner that evening when we were all in the drawing-room, Lady Catafalque dozing uneasily in her arm-chair behind a firescreen, and Chlorine, in the further room, playing funereal dirges in the darkness, and pressing the stiff keys of the old piano with a languid uncertain touch.

Drawing a chair up to Sir Paul's, I began to broach the subject calmly and temperately. 'I find,' I said, 'that we have not quite understood one another over this affair in the Grey Chamber. When I agreed to an appointment there, I thought—well, it doesn't matter what I thought, I was a little too premature. What I want to say now is, that while I have no objection to you, as Chlorine's father, asking me any questions (in reason) about myself, I feel a delicacy in discussing my private affairs with a perfect stranger.'

His burning eyes looked me through and through; 'I don't understand,' he said. 'Tell me what you are talking about.'

I began all over again, telling him exactly what I felt about solicitors and settlements. 'Are you well?' he asked sternly. 'What have I ever said about settlements or solicitors?

I saw that I was wrong again, and could only stammer something to the effect that a remark of Chlorine's had given me this impression.

'What she could have said to convey such an idea passes my comprehension,' he said gravely; 'but she knows nothing—she's a mere child. I have felt from the first, my boy, that your aunt's intention was to benefit you quite as much as my own daughter. Believe me, I shall not attempt to restrict you in any way; I shall be too rejoiced to see you come forth in safety from the Grey Chamber.'

All the relief I had begun to feel respecting the settlements was poisoned by these last words. Why did he talk of that confounded Grey Chamber as if it were a fiery furnace, or a cage of lions? What mystery was there concealed beneath all this, and how, since I was obviously supposed to be thoroughly acquainted with it, could I manage to penetrate the secret of this perplexing appointment?

While he had been speaking, the faint, mournful music died away, and, looking up, I saw Chlorine, a pale, slight form, standing framed in the archway which connected the two rooms.

'Go back to your piano, my child,' said the baronet; 'Augustus and I have much to talk about which is not for your ears.'

'But why not?' she said; 'oh, why not? Papa! dearest mother! Augustus! I can bear it no longer! I have often felt of late that we are living this strange life under the shadow of some fearful Thing, which would chase all cheerfulness from any home. More than this I did not seek to know; I dared not ask. But now, when I know that Augustus, whom I love with my whole heart, must shortly face this ghastly presence, you cannot wonder if I seek to learn the real extent of the danger that awaits him! Tell me all. I can bear the worst—for it cannot be more horrible than my own fears!'

Lady Catafalque had roused herself and was wringing her long mittened hands and moaning feebly. 'Paul,' she said, 'you must not tell her; it will kill her; she is not strong!' Her husband seemed undecided, and I myself began to feel exquisitely uncomfortable. Chlorine's words pointed to something infinitely more terrible than a mere solicitor.

'Poor girl,' said Sir Paul at last, 'it was for your own good that the whole truth has been thus concealed from you; but now, perhaps, the time has come when the truest kindness will be to reveal all. What do you say, Augustus?'

'I—I agree with you,' I replied faintly; 'she ought to be told.'

'Precisely!' he said. 'Break to her, then, the nature of the ordeal which lies before you.'

It was the very thing which I wanted to be broken to me! I would have given the world to know all about it myself, and so I stared at his gloomy old face with eyes that must have betrayed my helpless dismay. At last I saved myself by suggesting that such a story would come less harshly from a parent's lips.

'Well, so be it,' he said. 'Chlorine, compose yourself, dearest one; sit down there, and summon up all your fortitude to hear what I am about to tell you. You must know, then—I think you had better let your mother give you a cup of tea before I begin; it will steady your nerves.'

During the delay which followed—for Sir Paul did not consider his daughter sufficiently fortified until she had taken at least three cups—I suffered tortures of suspense, which I dared not betray.

They never thought of offering me any tea, though the merest observer might have noticed how very badly I wanted it.

At last the baronet was satisfied, and not without a sort of gloomy enjoyment and a proud relish of the distinction implied in his exceptional affliction, he began his weird and almost incredible tale.

'It is now,' said he, 'some centuries since our ill-fated house was first afflicted with the family curse which still attends it. A certain Humfrey de Catafalque, by his acquaintance with the black art, as it was said, had procured the services of a species of familiar, a dread and supernatural being. For some reason he had conceived a bitter enmity towards his nearest relations, whom he hated with a virulence that not even death could soften. For, by a refinement of malice, he bequeathed this baleful thing to his descendants for ever, as an inalienable heirloom! And to this day it follows the title—and the head of the family for the time being is bound to provide it with a secret apartment under his own roof. But that is not the worst: as each member of our house succeeds to the ancestral rank and honours, he must seek an interview with 'The Curse,' as it has been styled for generations. And, in that interview, it is decided whether the spell is to be broken and the Curse depart from us for ever—or whether it is to continue its blighting influence, and hold yet another life in miserable thraldom.'

'And are you one of its thralls then, papa?' faltered Chlorine.

'I am, indeed,' he said. 'I failed to quell it, as every Catafalque, however brave and resolute, has failed yet. It checks all my accounts, and woe to me if that cold, withering eye discovers the slightest error—even in the pence column! I could not describe the extent of my bondage to you, my daughter, or the humiliation of having to go and tremble monthly before that awful presence. Not even yet, old as I am, have I grown quite accustomed to it!'

Never, in my wildest imaginings, had I anticipated anything one quarter so dreadful as this; but still I clung to the hope that it was impossible to bring me into the affair.

'But, Sir Paul,' I said—'Sir Paul, you—you mustn't stop there, or you'll alarm Chlorine more than there's any need to do. She—ha, ha!—don't you see, she has got some idea into her head that I have to go through much the same sort of thing. Just explain that to her. I'm not a Catafalque, Chlorine, so it—it can't interfere with me. That is so, isn't it, Sir Paul? Good heavens, sir, don't torture her like this!' I cried, as he was silent. 'Speak out!'

'You mean well, Augustus,' he said, 'but the time for deceiving her has gone by; she must know the worst. Yes, my poor child,' he continued to Chlorine, whose eyes were wide with terror—though I fancy mine were even wider—'unhappily, though our beloved Augustus is not a Catafalque himself, he has of his own free will brought himself within the influence of the Curse, and he, too, at the appointed hour, must keep the awful assignation, and brave all that the most fiendish malevolence can do to shake his resolution.'

I could not say a single word; the horror of the idea was altogether too much for me, and I fell back on my chair in a state of speechless collapse.

'You see,' Sir Paul went on explaining, 'it is not only all new baronets, but every one who would seek an alliance with the females of our race, who must, by the terms of that strange bequest, also undergo this trial. It may be in some degree owing to this necessity that, ever since Humfrey de Catafalque's diabolical testament first took effect, every maiden of our House has died a spinster.' (Here Chlorine hid her face with a low wail.) 'In 1770, it is true, one solitary suitor was emboldened by love and daring to face the ordeal. He went calmly and resolutely to the chamber where the Curse was then lodged, and the next morning they found him outside the door—a gibbering maniac!'

I writhed on my chair. 'Augustus!' cried Chlorine wildly, 'promise me you will not permit the Curse to turn you into a gibbering maniac. I think if I saw you gibber I should die!'

I was on the verge of gibbering then; I dared not trust myself to speak.

'Nay, Chlorine,' said Sir Paul more cheerfully, 'there is no cause for alarm; all has been made smooth for Augustus.' (I began to brighten a little at this.) 'His Aunt Petronia had made a special study of the old-world science of incantation, and had undoubtedly succeeded at last in discovering the master-word which, employed according to her directions, would almost certainly break the unhallowed spell. In her compassionate attachment to us, she formed the design of persuading a youth of blameless life and antecedents to present himself as our champion, and the reports she had been given of our dear Augustus' irreproachable character led her to select him as a likely instrument. And her confidence in his generosity and courage was indeed well-founded, for he responded at once to the appeal of his departed aunt, and, with her instructions for his safeguard, and the consciousness of his virtue as an additional protection, there is hope, my child, strong hope, that, though the struggle may be a long and bitter one, yet Augustus will emerge a victor!'

I saw very little ground for expecting to emerge as anything of the kind, or for that matter to emerge at all, except in instalments,—for the master-word which was to abash the demon was probably inside the packet of instructions, and that was certainly somewhere at the bottom of the sea, outside Melbourne, fathoms below the surface.

I could bear no more. 'It's simply astonishing to me,' I said, 'that in the nineteenth century, hardly six miles from Charing Cross, you can calmly allow this hideous "Curse," or whatever you call it, to have things all its own way like this.'

'What can I do, Augustus?' he asked helplessly.

'Do? Anything!' I retorted wildly (for I scarcely knew what I said). 'Take it out for an airing (it must want an airing by this time); take it out—and lose it! Or get both the archbishops to step in and lay it for you. Sell the house, and make the purchaser take it at a valuation, with the other fixtures. I certainly would not live under the same roof with it. And I want you to understand one thing—I was never told all this; I have been kept in the dark about it. Of course I knew there was some kind of a curse in the family—but I never dreamed of anything so bad as this, and I never had any intention of being boxed up alone with it either. I shall not go near the Grey Chamber!'

'Not go near it!' they all cried aghast.

'Not on any account,' I said, for I felt firmer and easier now that I had taken up this position. 'If the Curse has any business with me, let it come down and settle it here before you all in a plain straightforward manner. Let us go about it in a business-like way. On second thoughts,' I added, fearing lest they should find means of carrying out this suggestion. 'I won't meet it anywhere!'

'And why—why won't you meet it?' they asked breathlessly.

'Because,' I explained desperately, 'because I'm—I'm a materialist.' (I had not been previously aware that I had any decided opinions on the question, but I could not stay then to consider the point.) 'How can I have any dealings with a preposterous supernatural something which my reason forbids me to believe in? You see my difficulty? It would be inconsistent, to begin with, and—and extremely painful to both sides.'

'No more of this ribaldry,' said Sir Paul sternly. 'It may be terribly remembered against you when the hour comes. Keep a guard over your tongue, for all our sakes, and more especially your own. Recollect that the Curse knows all that passes beneath this roof. And do not forget, too, that you are pledged—irrevocably pledged. You must confront the Curse!'

Only a short hour ago, and I had counted Chlorine's fortune and Chlorine as virtually mine; and now I saw my golden dreams roughly shattered for ever! And, oh, what a wrench it was to tear myself from them! what it cost me to speak the words that barred my Paradise to me for ever!

But if I wished to avoid confronting the Curse—and I did wish this very much—I had no other course. 'I had no right to pledge myself,' I said, with quivering lips, 'under all the circumstances.'

'Why not,' they demanded again; 'what circumstances?'

'Well, in the first place,' I assured them earnestly, 'I'm a base impostor. I am indeed. I'm not Augustus McFadden at all. My real name is of no consequence—but it's a prettier one than that. As for McFadden, he, I regret to say, is now no more.'

Why on earth I could not have told the plain truth here has always been a mystery to me. I suppose I had been lying so long that it was difficult to break myself of this occasionally inconvenient trick at so short a notice, but I certainly mixed things up to a hopeless extent.

'Yes,' I continued mournfully, 'McFadden is dead; I will tell you how he died if you would care to know. During his voyage here he fell overboard, and was almost instantly appropriated by a gigantic shark, when, as I happened to be present, I enjoyed the melancholy privilege of seeing him pass away. For one brief moment I beheld him between the jaws of the creature, so pale but so composed (I refer to McFadden, you understand—not the shark), he threw just one glance up at me, and with a smile, the sad sweetness of which I shall never forget (it was McFadden's smile, I mean, of course—not the shark's), he, courteous and considerate to the last, requested me to break the news and remember him very kindly to you all. And, in the same instant, he abruptly vanished within the monster—and I saw neither of them again!'

Of course in bringing the shark in at all I was acting directly contrary to my instructions, but I quite forgot them in my anxiety to escape the acquaintance of the Curse of the Catafalques.

'If this is true, sir,' said the baronet haughtily when I had finished, 'you have indeed deceived us basely.'

'That,' I replied, 'is what I was endeavouring to bring out. You see, it puts it quite out of my power to meet your family Curse. I should not feel justified in intruding upon it. So, if you will kindly let some one fetch a fly or a cab in half an hour—'

'Stop!' cried Chlorine. 'Augustus, as I will call you still, you must not go like this. If you have stooped to deceit, it was for love of me, and—and Mr. McFadden is dead. If he had been alive, I should have felt it my duty to allow him an opportunity of winning my affection, but he is lying in his silent tomb, and—and I have learnt to love you. Stay, then; stay and brave the Curse; we may yet be happy!'

I saw how foolish I had been not to tell the truth at first, and I hastened to repair this error. 'When I described McFadden as dead,' I said hoarsely, 'it was a loose way of putting the facts—because, to be quite accurate, he isn't dead. We found out afterwards that it was another fellow the shark had swallowed, and, in fact, another shark altogether. So he is alive and well now, at Melbourne, but when he came to know about the Curse, he was too much frightened to come across, and he asked me to call and make his excuses. I have now done so, and will trespass no further on your kindness—if you will tell somebody to bring a vehicle of any sort in a quarter of an hour.'

'Pardon me,' said the baronet, 'but we cannot part in this way. I feared when first I saw you that your resolution might give way under the strain; it is only natural, I admit. But you deceive yourself if you think we cannot see that these extraordinary and utterly contradictory stories are prompted by sudden panic. I quite understand it, Augustus; I cannot blame you; but to allow you to withdraw now would be worse than weakness on my part. The panic will pass, you will forget these fears to-morrow, you must forget them; remember, you have promised. For your own sake, I shall take care that you do not forfeit that solemn bond, for I dare not let you run the danger of exciting the Curse by a deliberate insult.'

I saw clearly that his conduct was dictated by a deliberate and most repulsive selfishness; he did not entirely believe me, but he was determined that if there was any chance that I, whoever I might be, could free him from his present thraldom, he would not let it escape him.

I raved, I protested, I implored—all in vain; they would not believe a single word I said, they positively refused to release me, and insisted upon my performing my engagement.

And at last Chlorine and her mother left the room, with a little contempt for my unworthiness mingled with their evident compassion; and a little later Sir Paul conducted me to my room, and locked me in 'till,' as he said, 'I had returned to my senses.'

IV.

What a night I passed, as I tossed sleeplessly from side to side under the canopy of my old-fashioned bedstead, torturing my fevered brain with vain speculations as to the fate the morrow was to bring me.

I felt myself perfectly helpless; I saw no way out of it; they seemed bent upon offering me up as a sacrifice to this private Moloch of theirs. The baronet was quite capable of keeping me locked up all the next day and pushing me into the Grey Chamber to take my chance when the hour came.

If I had only some idea what the Curse was like to look at, I thought I might not feel quite so afraid of it; the vague and impalpable awfulness of the thing was intolerable, and the very thought of it caused me to fling myself about in an ecstasy of horror.

By degrees, however, as daybreak came near, I grew calmer—until at length I arrived at a decision. It seemed evident to me that, as I could not avoid my fate, the wisest course was to go forth to meet it with as good a grace as possible. Then, should I by some fortunate accident come well out of it, my fortune was ensured.

But if I went on repudiating my assumed self to the very last, I should surely arouse a suspicion which the most signal rout of the Curse would not serve to dispel.

And after all, as I began to think, the whole thing had probably been much exaggerated; if I could only keep my head, and exercise all my powers of cool impudence, I might contrive to hoodwink this formidable relic of mediæval days, which must have fallen rather behind the age by this time. It might even turn out to be (although I was hardly sanguine as to this) as big a humbug as I was myself, and we should meet with confidential winks, like the two augurs.

But, at all events, I resolved to see this mysterious affair out, and trust to my customary good luck to bring me safely through, and so, having found the door unlocked, I came down to breakfast something like my usual self, and set myself to remove the unfavourable impression I had made on the previous night.

They did it from consideration for me, but still it was mistaken kindness for them all to leave me entirely to my own thoughts during the whole of the day, for I was driven to mope alone about the gloom-laden building, until by dinner-time I was very low indeed from nervous depression.

We dined in almost unbroken silence; now and then, as Sir Paul saw my hand approaching a decanter, he would open his lips to observe that I should need the clearest head and the firmest nerve ere long, and warn me solemnly against the brown sherry; from time to time, too, Chlorine and her mother stole apprehensive glances at me, and sighed heavily between every course. I never remember eating a dinner with so little enjoyment.

The meal came to an end at last; the ladies rose, and Sir Paul and I were left to brood over the dessert. I fancy both of us felt a delicacy in starting a conversation, and before I could hit upon a safe remark, Lady Catafalque and her daughter returned, dressed, to my unspeakable horror, in readiness to go out. Worse than that even, Sir Paul apparently intended to accompany them, for he rose at their entrance.

'It is now time for us to bid you a solemn farewell, Augustus,' he said, in his hollow old voice. 'You have three hours before you yet, and if you are wise, you will spend them in earnest self-preparation. At midnight, punctually, for you must not dare to delay, you will go to the Grey Chamber—the way thither you know, and you will find the Curse prepared for you. Good-bye, then, brave and devoted boy; stand firm, and no harm can befall you!'

'You are going away, all of you!' I cried. They were not what you might call a gay family to sit up with, but even their society was better than my own.

'Upon these dread occasions,' he explained, 'it is absolutely forbidden for any human being but one to remain in the house. All the servants have already left, and we are about to take our departure for a private hotel near the Strand. We shall just have time, if we start at once, to inspect the Soane Museum on our way thither, which will serve as some distraction from the terrible anxiety we shall be feeling.'

At this I believe I positively howled with terror; all my old panic came back with a rush. 'Don't leave me all alone with It!' I cried; 'I shall go mad if you do!'

Sir Paul simply turned on his heel in silent contempt, and his wife followed him; but Chlorine remained behind for one instant, and somehow, as she gazed at me with a yearning pity in her sad eyes, I thought I had never seen her looking so pretty before.

'Augustus,' she said, 'get up.' (I suppose I must have been on the floor somewhere.) 'Be a man; show us we were not mistaken in you. You know I would spare you this if I could; but we are powerless. Oh, be brave, or I shall lose you for ever!'

Her appeal did seem to put a little courage into me, I staggered up and kissed her slender hand and vowed sincerely to be worthy of her.

And then she too passed out, and the heavy hall door slammed behind the three, and the rusty old gate screeched like a banshee as it swung back and closed with a clang.

I heard the carriage-wheels grind the slush, and the next moment I knew that I was shut up on Christmas Eve in that sombre mansion—with the Curse of the Catafalques as my sole companion!

I don't think the generous ardour with which Chlorine's last words had inspired me lasted very long, for I caught myself shivering before the clock struck nine, and, drawing up a clumsy leathern arm-chair close to the fire, I piled on the logs and tried to get rid of a certain horrible sensation of internal vacancy which was beginning to afflict me.

I tried to look my situation fairly in the face; whatever reason and common sense had to say about it, there seemed no possible doubt that something of a supernatural order was shut up in that great chamber down the corridor, and also that, if I meant to win Chlorine, I must go up and have some kind of an interview with it. Once more I wished I had some definite idea to go upon; what description of being should I find this Curse? Would it be aggressively ugly, like the bogie of my infancy, or should I see a lank and unsubstantial shape, draped in clinging black, with nothing visible beneath it but a pair of burning hollow eyes and one long pale bony hand? Really I could not decide which would be the more trying of the two.

By-and-by I began to recollect unwillingly all the frightful stories I had ever read; one in particular came back to me,—the adventure of a foreign marshal who, after much industry, succeeded in invoking an evil spirit, which came bouncing into the room shaped like a gigantic ball, with, I think, a hideous face in the middle of it, and would not be got rid of until the horrified marshal had spent hours in hard praying and persistent exorcism!

What should I do if the Curse was a globular one and came rolling all round the room after me?

Then there was another appalling tale I had read in some magazine,—a tale of a secret chamber, too, and in some respects a very similar case to my own, for there the heir of some great house had to go in and meet a mysterious aged person with strange eyes and an evil smile, who kept attempting to shake hands with him.

Nothing should induce me to shake hands with the Curse of the Catafalques, however apparently friendly I might find it.

But it was not very likely to be friendly, for it was one of those mystic powers of darkness which know nearly everything—it would detect me as an impostor directly, and what would become of me? I declare I almost resolved to confess all and sob out my deceit upon its bosom, and the only thing which made me pause was the reflection that probably the Curse did not possess a bosom.

By this time I had worked myself up to such a pitch of terror that I found it absolutely necessary to brace my nerves, and I did brace them. I emptied all the three decanters, but as Sir Paul's cellar was none of the best, the only result was that, while my courage and daring were not perceptibly heightened, I was conscious of feeling exceedingly unwell.

Tobacco, no doubt, would have calmed and soothed me, but I did not dare to smoke. For the Curse, being old-fashioned, might object to the smell of it, and I was anxious to avoid exciting its prejudices unnecessarily.

And so I simply sat in my chair and shook. Every now and then I heard steps on the frosty path outside: sometimes a rapid tread, as of some happy person bound to scenes of Christmas revelry, and little dreaming of the miserable wretch he was passing; sometimes the slow creaking tramp of the Fulham policeman on his beat.

What if I called him in and gave the Curse into custody—either for putting me in bodily fear (as it was undeniably doing), or for being found on the premises under suspicious circumstances?

There was a certain audacity about this means of cutting the knot that fascinated me at first, but still I did not venture to adopt it, thinking it most probable that the stolid constable would decline to interfere as soon as he knew the facts; and even if he did, it would certainly annoy Sir Paul extremely to hear of his Family Curse spending its Christmas in a police-cell, and I felt instinctively that he would consider it a piece of unpardonable bad taste on my part.

So one hour passed. A few minutes after ten I heard more footsteps and voices in low consultation, as if a band of men had collected outside the railings. Could there be any indication without of the horrors these walls contained?

But no; the gaunt house-front kept its secret too well; they were merely the waits. They saluted me with the old carol, 'God rest you, merry gentleman, let nothing you dismay!' which should have encouraged me, but it didn't, and they followed that up by a wheezy but pathetic rendering of 'The Mistletoe Bough.'

For a time I did not object to them; while they were scraping and blowing outside I felt less abandoned and cut off from human help, and then they might arouse softer sentiments in the Curse upstairs by their seasonable strains: these things do happen at Christmas sometimes. But their performance was really so infernally bad that it was calculated rather to irritate than subdue any evil spirit, and very soon I rushed to the window and beckoned to them furiously to go away.

Unhappily, they thought I was inviting them indoors for refreshment, and came round to the gate, when they knocked and rang incessantly for a quarter of an hour.

This must have stirred the Curse up quite enough, but when they had gone, there came a man with a barrel organ, which was suffering from some complicated internal disorder, causing it to play its whole repertory at once, in maddening discords. Even the grinder himself seemed dimly aware that his instrument was not doing itself justice, for he would stop occasionally, as if to ponder or examine it. But he was evidently a sanguine person and had hopes of bringing it round by a little perseverance; so, as Parson's Green was well-suited by its quiet for this mode of treatment, he remained there till he must have reduced the Curse to a rampant and rabid condition.

He went at last, and then the silence that followed began to my excited fancy (for I certainly saw nothing) to be invaded by strange sounds that echoed about the old house. I heard sharp reports from the furniture, sighing moans in the draughty passages, doors opening and shutting, and—worse still— stealthy padding footsteps, both above and in the ghostly hall outside!

I sat there in an ice-cold perspiration, until my nerves required more bracing, to effect which I had recourse to the spirit-case.

And after a short time my fears began to melt away rapidly. What a ridiculous bugbear I was making of this thing after all! Was I not too hasty in setting it down as ugly and hostile before I had seen it ... how did I know it was anything which deserved my horror?

Here a gush of sentiment came over me at the thought that it might be that for long centuries the poor Curse had been cruelly misunderstood—that it might be a blessing in disguise.

I was so affected by the thought that I resolved to go up at once and wish it a merry Christmas through the keyhole, just to show that I came in no unfriendly spirit.

But would not that seem as if I was afraid of it? I scorned the idea of being afraid. Why, for two straws, I would go straight in and pull its nose for it—if it had a nose!

I went out with this object, not very steadily, but before I had reached the top of the dim and misty staircase, I had given up all ideas of defiance, and merely intended to go as far as the corridor by way of a preliminary canter.

The coffin-lid door stood open, and I looked apprehensively down the corridor; the grim metal fittings on the massive door of the Grey Chamber were gleaming with a mysterious pale light, something between the phenomena obtained by electricity and the peculiar phosphorescence observable in a decayed shell-fish; under the door I saw the reflection of a sullen red glow, and within I could hear sounds like the roar of a mighty wind, above which peals of fiendish mirth rang out at intervals, and were followed by a hideous dull clanking.

It seemed only too evident that the Curse was getting up the steam for our interview. I did not stay there long, because I was afraid that it might dart out suddenly and catch me eavesdropping, which would be a hopelessly bad beginning. I got back to the dining-room, somehow; the fire had taken advantage of my short absence to go out, and I was surprised to find by the light of the fast-dimming lamp that it was a quarter to twelve already.

Only fifteen more fleeting minutes and then—unless I gave up Chlorine and her fortune for ever—I must go up and knock at that awful door, and enter the presence of the frightful mystic Thing that was roaring and laughing and clanking on the other side!

Stupidly I sat and stared at the clock; in five minutes, now, I should be beginning my desperate duel with one of the powers of darkness—a thought which gave me sickening qualms.

I was clinging to the thought that I had still two precious minutes left—perhaps my last moments of safety and sanity—when the lamp expired with a gurgling sob, and left me in the dark.

I was afraid of sitting there all alone any longer, and besides, if I lingered, the Curse might come down and fetch me. The horror of this idea made me resolve to go up at once, especially as scrupulous punctuality might propitiate it.

Groping my way to the door, I reached the hall and stood there, swaying under the old stained-glass lantern. And then I made a terrible discovery. I was not in a condition to transact any business; I had disregarded Sir Paul's well-meant warning at dinner; I was not my own master. I was lost!

The clock in the adjoining room tolled twelve, and from without the distant steeples proclaimed in faint peals and chimes that it was Christmas morn. My hour had come!

Why did I not mount those stairs? I tried again and again, and fell down every time, and at each attempt I knew the Curse would be getting more and more impatient.

I was quite five minutes late, and yet, with all my eagerness to be punctual, I could not get up that staircase. It was a horrible situation, but it was not at its worst even then, for I heard a jarring sound above, as if heavy rusty bolts were being withdrawn.

The Curse was coming down to see what had become of me! I should have to confess my inability to go upstairs without assistance, and so place myself wholly at its mercy!

I made one more desperate effort, and then—and then, upon my word, I don't know how it was exactly—but, as I looked wildly about, I caught sight of my hat on the hat-rack below, and the thoughts it roused in me proved too strong for resistance. Perhaps it was weak of me, but I venture to think that very few men in my position would have behaved any better.

I renounced my ingenious and elaborate scheme for ever, the door (fortunately for me) was neither locked nor bolted, and the next moment I was running for my life along the road to Chelsea, urged on by the fancy that the Curse itself was in hot pursuit.

For weeks after that I lay in hiding, starting at every sound, so fearful was I that the outraged Curse might track me down at last; all my worldly possessions were at Parson's Green, and I could not bring myself to write or call for them, nor indeed have I seen any of the Catafalques since that awful Christmas Eve.

I wish to have nothing more to do with them, for I feel naturally that they took a cruel advantage of my youth and inexperience, and I shall always resent the deception and constraint to which I so nearly fell a victim.

But it occurs to me that those who may have followed my strange story with any curiosity and interest may be slightly disappointed at its conclusion, which I cannot deny is a lame and unsatisfactory one.

They expected, no doubt, to be told what the Curse's personal appearance is, and how it comports itself in that ghastly Grey Chamber, what it said to me, and what I said to it, and what happened after that.

This information, as will be easily understood, I cannot pretend to give, and, for myself, I have long ceased to feel the slightest curiosity on any of these points. But for the benefit of such as are less indifferent, I may suggest that almost any eligible bachelor would easily obtain the opportunities I failed to enjoy by simply calling at the old mansion at Parson's Green, and presenting himself to the baronet as a suitor for his daughter's hand.

I shall be most happy to allow my name to be used as a reference.

Marjory

I have thought myself justified in printing the following narrative, found among the papers of my dead friend, Douglas Cameron, who left me discretion to deal with them as I saw fit. It was written indeed, as its opening words imply, rather for his own solace and relief than with the expectation that it would be read by any other. But, painful and intimate as it is in parts, I cannot think that any harm will be done by printing it now, with some necessary alterations in the names of the characters chiefly concerned.

Before, however, leaving the story to speak for itself, I should like to state, in justice to my friend, that during the whole of my acquaintance with him, which began in our college days, I never saw anything to indicate the morbid timidity and weakness of character that seem to have marked him as a boy. Reserved he undoubtedly was, with a taste for solitude that made him shrink from the society of all but a small circle, and with a sensitive and shy nature which prevented him from doing himself complete justice; but he was very capable of holding his own on occasion, and in his disposition, as I knew it, there was no want of moral courage, nor any trace of effeminacy.

How far he may have unconsciously exaggerated such failings in the revelation of his earlier self, or what the influence of such an experience as he relates may have done to strengthen the moral fibre, are points on which I can express no opinion, any more than I can pledge myself to the credibility of the supernatural element of his story.

It may be that only in the boy's overwrought imagination, the innocent Child-spirit came back to complete the work of love and pity she had begun in life; but I know that he himself believed otherwise, and, truly, if those who leave us are permitted to return at all, it must be on some such errand as Marjory's.

Douglas Cameron's life was short, and in it, so far as I am aware, he met no one who at all replaced his lost ideal. Of this I cannot be absolutely certain, for he was a reticent man in such matters; but I think, had it been so, I should have known of it, for we were very close friends. One would hardly expect, perhaps, that an ordinary man would remain faithful all his days to the far-off memory of a child-love; but then Cameron was not quite as other men, nor were his days long in the land.

And if this ideal of his was never dimmed for him by some grosser, and less spiritual, passion, who shall say that he may not have been a better and even a happier man in consequence.

It is not without an effort that I have resolved to break, in the course of this narrative, the reserve maintained for nearly twenty years. But the chief reason for silence is removed now that all those are gone who might have been pained or harmed by what I have to tell, and, though I shrink still from reviving certain memories that are fraught with pain, there are others associated therewith which will surely bring consolation and relief.

I must have been about eleven at the time I am speaking of, and the change which—for good or ill—comes over most boys' lives had not yet threatened mine. I had not left home for school, nor did it seem at all probable then that I should ever do so.

When I read (I was a great reader) of Dotheboys Hall and Salem House—a combination of which establishments formed my notion of school-life—it was with no more personal interest than a cripple might feel in perusing the notice of an impending conscription; for from the battles of school-life I was fortunately exempted.

I was the only son of a widow, and we led a secluded life in a London suburb. My mother took charge of my education herself, and, as far as mere acquirements went, I was certainly not behind other boys of my age. I owe too much to that loving and careful training, Heaven knows, to think of casting any reflection upon it here, but my surroundings were such as almost necessarily to exclude all bracing and hardening influences.

My mother had few friends; we were content with our own companionship, and of boys I knew and cared to know nothing; in fact, I regarded a strange boy with much the same unreasoning aversion as many excellent women feel for the most ordinary cow.

I was happy to think that I should never be called upon to associate with them; by-and-by, when I outgrew my mother's teaching, I was to have a tutor, perhaps even go to college in time, and when I became a man I was to be a curate and live with my mother in a clematis-covered cottage in some pleasant village.

She would often dwell on this future with a tender prospective pride; she spoke of it on the very day that saw it shattered for ever.

For there came a morning when, on going to her with my lessons for the day, I was gladdened with an unexpected holiday. I little knew then—though I was to learn it soon enough—that my lessons had been all holidays, or that on that day they were to end for ever.

My mother had had one or two previous attacks of an illness which seemed to prostrate her for a short period, and as she soon regained her ordinary health, I did not think they could be of a serious nature.

So I devoted my holiday cheerfully enough to the illumination of a text, on the gaudy colouring of which I found myself gazing two days later with a dull wonder, as at the work of a strange hand in a long dead past, for the boy who had painted that was a happy boy who had a mother, and for two endless days I had been alone.

Those days, and many that followed, come back to me now but vaguely. I passed them mostly in a state of blank bewilderment caused by the double sense of sameness and strangeness in everything around me; then there were times when this gave way to a passionate anguish which refused all attempts at comfort, and times even—but very, very seldom—when I almost forgot what had happened to me.

Our one servant remained in the house with me, and a friend and neighbour of my mother's was constant in her endeavours to relieve my loneliness; but I was impatient of them, I fear, and chiefly anxious to be left alone to indulge my melancholy unchecked.

I remember how, as autumn began, and leaf after leaf fluttered down from the trees in our little garden, I watched them fall with a heavier heart, for they had known my mother, and now they, too, were deserting me.

This morbid state of mind had lasted quite long enough when my uncle, who was my guardian, saw fit to put a summary end to it by sending me to school forthwith; he would have softened the change for me by taking me to his own home first, but there was illness of some sort there, and this was out of the question.

I was neither sorry nor glad when I heard of it, for all places were the same to me just then; only, as the time drew near, I began to regard the future with a growing dread.

The school was at some distance from London, and my uncle took me down by rail; but the only fact I remember connected with the journey is that there was a boy in the carriage with us who cracked walnuts all the way, and I wondered if he was going to school too, and concluded that he was not, or he would hardly eat quite so many walnuts.

Later we were passing through some wrought-iron gates, and down an avenue of young chestnuts, which made a gorgeous autumn canopy of scarlet, amber, and orange, up to a fine old red-brick house, with a high-pitched roof, and a cupola in which a big bell hung, tinted a warm gold by the afternoon sun.

This was my school, and it did not look so very-terrible after all. There was a big bow-window by the pillared portico, and, looking timidly in, I saw a girl of about my own age sitting there, absorbed in the book she was reading, her long brown hair drooping over her cheek and the hand on which it rested.

She glanced up at the sound of the door-bell, and I felt her eyes examining me seriously and critically, and then I forgot everything but the fact that I was about to be introduced to my future schoolmaster, the Rev. Basil Dering.

This was less of an ordeal than I had expected; he had a strong, massively-cut, leonine face, free and abundant white hair, streaked with dark grey, but there was a kind light in his eyes as I looked up at them, and the firm mouth could smile, I found, pleasantly enough.

Mrs. Dering seemed younger, and was handsome, with a certain stateliness and decision of manner which put me less at my ease, and I was relieved to be told I might say good-bye to my uncle, and wander about the grounds as I liked.

I was not surprised to pass through an empty schoolroom, and to descend by some steep stairs to a deserted playground, for we had been already told that the Michaelmas holidays were not over, and that the boys would not return for some days to come.

It gave me a kind of satisfaction to think of my resemblance, just then, to my favourite David Copperfield, but I was to have a far pleasanter companion than poor lugubrious, flute-tootling Mr. Mell, for as I paced the damp paths paved with a mosaic of russet and yellow leaves, I heard light footsteps behind me, and turned to find myself face to face with the girl I had seen at the window.

She stood there breathless for an instant, for she had hurried to overtake me, and against a background of crimson creepers I saw the brilliant face, with its soft but fearless brown eyes, small straight nose, spirited mouth, and crisp wavy golden-brown hair, which I see now almost as distinctly as I write.

'You're the new boy,' she said at length. 'I've come out to make you feel more at home. I suppose you don't feel quite at home just yet?'

'Not quite, thank you,' I said, lifting my cap with ceremony, for I had been taught to be particular about my manners; 'I have never been to school before, you see, Miss Dering.'

I think she was a little puzzled by so much politeness. 'I know,' she said softly; 'mother told me about it, and I'm very sorry. And I'm called Marjory, generally. Shall you like school, do you think?'

'I might,' said I, 'if—if it wasn't for the boys!'

'Boys aren't bad,' she said; 'ours are rather nice, I think. But perhaps you don't know many?'

'I know one,' I replied.

'How old is he?' she wished to know.

'Not very old—about three, I think,' I said. I had never wished till then that my only male acquaintance had been of less tender years, but I felt now that he was rather small, and saw that Marjory was of the same opinion.

'Why, he's only a baby!' she said; 'I thought you meant a real boy. And is that all the boys you know? Are you fond of games?'

'Some games—very,' said I.

'What's your favourite game?' she demanded.

'Bezique,' I answered, 'or draughts.'

'I meant outdoor games; draughts are indoor games—is indoor games, I mean—no, are an indoor game—and that doesn't sound grammar! But haven't you ever played cricket? Not ever, really? I like it dreadfully myself, only I'm not allowed to play with the boys, and I'm sure I can bat well enough for the second eleven—Cartwright said I could last term—and I can bowl round-hand, and it's all no use, just because I was born a girl! Wouldn't you like a game at something? They haven't taken in the croquet hoops yet; shall we play at that?'

But again I had to confess my ignorance of what was then the popular garden game.

'What do you generally do to amuse yourself, then?' she inquired.

'I read, generally, or paint texts or outlines. Sometimes'—(I thought this accomplishment would surely appeal to her)—'sometimes I do woolwork!'

'I don't think I would tell the boys that,' she advised rather gravely; she evidently considered me a very desperate case. 'It's such a pity, your not knowing any games. Suppose I taught you croquet, now? It would be something to go on with, and you'll soon learn if you pay attention and do exactly what I tell you.'

I submitted myself meekly to her direction, and Marjory enjoyed her office of instructress for a time, until my extreme slowness wore out her patience, and she began to make little murmurs of disgust, for which she invariably apologised. 'That's enough for to-day!' she said at last, 'I'll take you again to-morrow. But you really must try and pick up games, Cameron, or you'll never be liked. Let me see, I wonder if there's time to teach you a little football. I think I could do that.'

Before she could make any further arrangements the tea-bell rang, but when I lay down that night in my strange cold bed, hemmed round by other beds, which were only less formidable than if they had been occupied, I did not feel so friendless as I might have done, and dreamed all night that Marjory was teaching me something I understood to be cricket, which, however, was more like a bloated kind of backgammon.

The next day Marjory was allowed to go out walking with me, and I came home feeling that I had known her for quite a long time, while her manner to me had acquired a tone even more protecting than before, and she began to betray an anxiety as to my school prospects which filled me with uneasiness.

'I am so afraid the boys won't like the way you talk,' she said on one occasion.

'I used to be told I spoke very correctly,' I said, verdantly enough.

'But not like boys talk. You see, Cameron, I ought to know, with such a lot of them about. I tell you what I could do, though—I could teach you most of their words—only I must run and ask mother first if I may. Teaching slang isn't the same as using it on my own account, is it?'

Marjory darted off impulsively to ask leave, to return presently with a slow step and downcast face. 'I mayn't,' she announced. 'Mother says "Certainly not," so there's an end of that! Still, I think myself it's a decided pity.'

And more than once that day she would observe, as if to herself, 'I do wish they had let him come to school in different collars!'

I knew that these remarks, and others of a similar tendency, were prompted by her interest in my welfare, and I admired her too heartily already to be offended by them: still, I cannot say they added to my peace of mind.

And on the last evening of the holidays she said 'Good-night' to me with some solemnity. 'Everything will be different after this,' she said; 'I shan't be able to see nearly so much of you, because I'm not allowed to be much with the boys. But I shall be looking after you all the time, Cameron, and seeing how you get on. And oh! I do hope you will try to be a popular kind of boy!'

I'm afraid I must own that this desire of Marjory's was not realised. I do not know that I tried to be—and I certainly was not—a popular boy.

The other boys, I now know, were by no means bad specimens of the English schoolboy, as will be evident when I state that, for a time, my deep mourning was held by them to give me a claim to their forbearance.

But I had an unfortunate tendency to sudden floods of tears (apparently for no cause whatever, really from some secret spring of association, such as I remember was touched when I first found myself learning Latin from the same primer over which my mother and I had puzzled together), and these outbursts at first aroused my companions' contempt, and finally their open ridicule.

I could not conceal my shrinking dislike to their society, which was not calculated to make them more favourably disposed towards me; while my tastes, my expressions, my ways of looking at things, were all at total variance with their own standards.

The general disapproval might well have shown itself in a harsher manner than that of merely ignoring my existence—and it says much for the tone of the school that it did not; unfortunately, I felt their indifference almost as keenly as I had dreaded their notice.

From my masters I met with more favour, for I had been thoroughly well grounded, and found, besides, a temporary distraction in my school-work; but this was hardly likely to render me more beloved by my fellows, and so it came to pass that every day saw my isolation more complete.

Something, however, made me anxious to hide this from Marjory's eyes, and whenever she happened to be looking on at us in the school grounds or the playing fields, I made dismal attempts to appear on terms of equality with the rest, and would hang about a group with as much pretence of belonging to it as I thought at all prudent.

If she had had more opportunities of questioning me, she would have found me out long before; as it was, the only occasion on which we were near one another was at the weekly drawing lesson, when, although she drew less and talked more than the Professor quite approved of, she was obliged to restrict herself to a conversation which did not admit of confidences.

But this negative neutral-tinted misery was not to last; I was harmless enough, but then to some natures nothing is so offensive as inoffensiveness. My isolation was certain to raise me up an enemy in time, and he came in the person of one Clarence Ormsby.

He was a sturdy, good-looking fellow, about two years older than myself, good at games, and, though not brilliant in other respects, rather idle than dull. He was popular in the school, and I believe his general disposition was by no means bad; but there must have been some hidden flaw in his nature which might never have disclosed itself for any other but me.

For me he had displayed, almost from the first, one of those special antipathies that want but little excuse to ripen into hatred. My personal appearance—I had the misfortune to be a decidedly plain boy—happened to be particularly displeasing to him, and, as he had an unsparing tongue, he used it to cover me with ridicule, until gradually, finding that I did not retaliate, he indulged in acts of petty oppression which, though not strictly bullying, were even more harassing and humiliating.

I suspect now that if I had made ever so slight a stand at the outset, I should have escaped further molestation, but I was not pugnacious by nature, and never made the experiment; partly, probably, from a theory on which I had been reared, that all violence was vulgar, but chiefly from a tendency, unnatural in one of my age and sex, to find a sentimental satisfaction in a certain degree of unhappiness.

So that I can neither pity myself nor expect pity from others for woes which were so essentially my own creation, though they resulted, alas! in misery that was real enough.

It was inevitable that quick-sighted Marjory should discover the subjection into which I had fallen, and her final enlightenment was brought about in this manner. Ormsby and I were together alone, shortly before morning school, and he came towards me with an exercise of mine from which he had just been copying his own, for we were in the same classes, despite the difference in our ages, and he was in the habit of profiting thus by my industry.

'Thanks, Cameron,' he said, with a sweetness which I distrusted, for he was not as a rule so lavish in his gratitude. 'I've copied out that exercise of yours, but it's written so beastly badly that you'd better do it over again.'

With which he deliberately tore the page he had been copying from to scraps, which he threw in my face, and strolled out down to the playground.

I was preparing submissively to do the exercise over again as well as I could in the short time that was left, when I was startled by a low cry of indignation, and, looking round, saw Marjory standing in the doorway, and knew by her face that she had seen all.

'Has Ormsby done that to you before?' she inquired.

'Once or twice he has,' said I.

'And you let him!' she cried. 'Oh, Cameron!'

'What can I do?' I said.

'I know what I would do,' she replied. 'I would slap his face, or pinch him. I wouldn't put up with it!'

'Boys don't slap one another, or pinch,' I said, not displeased to find a weak place in her knowledge of us.

'Well, they do something!' she said; 'a real boy would. But I don't think you are a real boy, Cameron. I'll show you what to do. Where's the exercise that—that pig copied? Ah! I see it. And now—look!' (Here she tore his page as he had torn mine.)

'Now for an envelope!' and from the Doctor's own desk she took an envelope, in which she placed the fragments, and wrote on the outside in her round, childish hand: 'With Marjory's compliments, for being a bully.'

'He won't do that again,' she said gleefully.

'He'll do worse,' I said in dismay; 'I shall have to pay for it. Marjory, why didn't you leave things alone? I didn't complain—you know I didn't.'

She turned upon me, as well she might, in supreme disdain. 'Oh! what a coward you are! I wouldn't believe all Cartwright told me about you when I asked—but I see it's all true. Why don't you stick up for yourself?'

I muttered something or other.

'But you ought to. You'll never get on unless,' said Marjory, very decidedly. 'Now, promise me you will, next time.'

I sat there silent. I was disgusted with myself, and meanly angry with her for having rendered me so.

'Then, listen,' she said impressively. 'I promised I would look after you, and I did mean to, but it's no use if you won't help yourself. So, unless you say you won't go on being a coward any more, I shall have to leave you to your own way, and not take the least interest in you ever again.'

'Then, you may,' I said stolidly; 'I don't care.' I wondered, even while I spoke the words, what could be impelling me to treat spirited, warm-hearted Marjory like that, and I hate myself still at the recollection.

'Good-bye, then,' she said very quietly; 'I'm sorry, Cameron.' And she went out without another word.

When Ormsby came in, I watched him apprehensively as he read the envelope upon his desk and saw its contents. He said nothing, however, though he shot a malignant glance in my direction; but the lesson was not lost upon him, for from that time he avoided all open ill-treatment of me, and even went so far as to assume a friendliness which might have reassured me had I not instinctively felt that it merely masked the old dislike.

I was constantly the victim of mishaps, in the shape of missing and defaced books, ink mysteriously spilt or strangely adulterated, and, though I could never trace them to any definite hand, they seemed too systematic to be quite accidental; still I made no sign, and hoped thus to disarm my persecutor—if persecutor there were.

As for my companions, I knew that in no case would they take the trouble to interfere in my behalf; they had held aloof from the first, the general opinion (which I now perceive was not unjust) being that 'I deserved all I got.'

And my estrangement from Marjory grew wider and wider; she never spoke to me now when we sat near one another at the drawing-class; if she looked at me it was by stealth, and with a glance that I thought sometimes was contemptuously pitiful, and sometimes half fancied betrayed a willingness to return to the old comradeship.

But I nursed my stupid, sullen pride, though my heart ached with it at times. For I had now come to love Marjory devotedly, with a love that, though I was a boy and she was a child, was as genuine as any I am ever likely to feel again.

The chance of seeing her now and then, of hearing her speak—though it was not to me—gave me the one interest in my life, which, but for her, I could hardly have borne. But this love of mine was a very far-off and disinterested worship after all. I could not imagine myself ever speaking of it to her, or picture her as accepting it. Marjory was too thorough a child to be vulgarised in that way, even in thought.

The others were healthy, matter-of-fact youths, to whom Marjory was an ordinary girl, and who certainly did not indulge in any strained sentiment respecting her; it was left for me to idealise her; but of that, at least, I cannot feel ashamed, or believe that it did me anything but good.

And the days went on, until it wanted but a fortnight to Christmas, and most of us were thinking of the coming holidays, and preparing with a not unpleasant excitement for the examinations, which were all that barred the way to them now. I was to spend my Christmas with my uncle and cousins, who would by that time be able to receive me; but I felt no very pleasurable anticipations, for my cousins were all boys, and from boys I thought I knew what to expect.

One afternoon Ormsby came to me with the request that I would execute a trifling commission for him in the adjoining village; he himself, he said, was confined to bounds, but he had a shilling he wanted to lay out at a small fancy-shop we were allowed to patronise, and he considered me the best person to be entrusted with that coin. I was simply to spend the money on anything I thought best, for he had entire confidence, he gave me to understand, in my taste and judgment. I think I suspected a design of some sort, but I did not dare to refuse, and then his manner to some extent disarmed me.

I took the shilling, therefore, with which I bought some article—I forget what—and got back to the school at dusk. The boys had all gone down to tea except Ormsby, who was waiting for me up in the empty schoolroom.

'Well?' he said, and I displayed my purchase, only to find that I had fallen into a trap.

When I think how easily I was the dupe of that not too subtle artifice, which was only half malicious, I could smile, if I did not know how it ended.

'How much was that?' he asked contemptuously, 'twopence-halfpenny? Well, if you choose to give a shilling for it, I'm not going to pay, that's all. So just give me back my shilling!'

Now, as my weekly allowance consisted of threepence, which was confiscated for some time in advance (as I think he knew), to provide fines for my mysteriously-stained dictionaries, this was out of the question, as I represented.

'Then go back to the shop and change it,' said he; 'I won't have that thing!'

'Tell me what you would like instead, and I will,' I stipulated, not unreasonably.

He laughed; his little scheme was working so admirably. 'That's not the bargain,' he said; 'you're bound to get me something I like. I'm not obliged to tell you what it is.'

But even I was driven to protest against such flagrant unfairness. 'I didn't know you meant that,' I said, 'or I'm sure I shouldn't have gone. I went to oblige you, Ormsby.'

'No, you didn't,' he said, 'you went because I told you. And you'll go again.'

'Not unless you tell me what I'm to get,' I said.

'I tell you what I believe,' he said; 'you never spent the whole shilling at all on that; you bought something for yourself with the rest, you young swindler! No wonder you won't go back to the shop.'

This was, of course, a mere taunt flung out by his inventive fancy; but as he persisted in it, and threatened exposure and a variety of consequences, I became alarmed, for I had little doubt that, innocent as I was, I could be made very uncomfortable by accusations which would find willing hearers.

He stood there enjoying my perplexity and idly twisting a piece of string round and round his fingers. At length he said, 'Well, I don't want to be hard on you. You may go and change this for me even now, if you like. I'll give you three minutes to think it over, and you can come down into the playground when I sing out, and tell me what you mean to do. And you had better be sharp in coming, too, or it will be the worse for you.'

He took his cap, and presently I heard him going down the steps to the playground. I would have given worlds to go and join the rest at tea, but I did not dare, and remained in the schoolroom, which was dim just then, for the gas was lowered; and while I stood there by the fireplace, trembling in the cold air which stole in through the door Ormsby had left open, Marjory came in by the other one, and was going straight to her father's desk, when she saw me.

Her first impulse seemed to be to take no notice, but something in my face or attitude made her alter her mind and come straight to me, holding out her hand.

'Cameron,' she said, 'shall we be friends again?'

'Yes, Marjory,' I said; I could not have said any more just then.

'You look so miserable, I couldn't bear it any longer,' she said, 'so I had to make it up. You know, I was only pretending crossness, Cameron, all the time, because I really thought it was best. But it doesn't seem to have done you much good, and I did promise to take care of you. What is it? Ormsby again?'

'Yes,' I said, and told her the story of the commission.

'Oh, you stupid boy!' she cried, 'couldn't you see he only wanted to pick a quarrel? And if you change it now, he'll make you change it again, and the next time, and the next after that—I know he will!'

Here Ormsby's voice shouted from below, 'Now then, you, Cameron, time's up!'

'What is he doing down there?' asked Marjory, and her indignation rose higher when she heard.

'Now, Cameron, be brave; go down and tell him once for all he may just keep what he has, and be thankful. Whatever it is, it's good enough for him, I'm sure!'

But I still hung back. 'It's no use, Marjory, he'll tell everyone I cheated him—he says he will!'

'That he shall not!' she cried; 'I won't have it, I'll go myself, and tell him what I think of him, and make him stop treating you like this.'

Some faint glimmer of manliness made me ashamed to allow her thus to fight my battles. 'No, Marjory, not you!' I said; 'I will go: I'll say what you want me to say!'

But it was too late. I saw her for just a second at the door, my impetuous, generous little Marjory, as she flung back her pretty hair in a certain spirited way she had, and nodded to me encouragingly.

And then—I can hardly think of it calmly even now—there came a sharp scream, and the sound of a fall, and, after that, silence.

Sick with fear, I rushed to the head of the steps, and looked down into the brown gloom.

'Keep where you are for a minute!' I heard Ormsby cry out. 'It's all right—she's not hurt; now you can come down.'

I was down in another instant, at the foot of the stairs, where, in a patch of faint light that fell from the door above, lay Marjory, with Ormsby bending over her insensible form.

'She's dead!' I cried in my terror, as I saw her white face.

'I tell you she's all right,' said he, impatiently; 'there's nothing to make a fuss about. She slipped coming down and cut her forehead—that's all.'

'Marjory, speak to me—don't look like that; tell me you're not much hurt!' I implored her; but she only moaned a little, and her eyes remained fast shut.

'It's no use worrying her now, you know,' said Ormsby, more gently. 'Just help me to get her round to the kitchen door, and tell somebody.'

We carried her there between us, and, amidst a scene of terrible confusion and distress, Marjory, still insensible, was carried into the library, and a man sent off in hot haste for the surgeon.

A little later Ormsby and I were sent for to the study, where Dr. Dering, whose face was white and drawn as I had never seen it before, questioned us closely as to our knowledge of the accident.

Ormsby could only say that he was out in the playground, when he saw somebody descending the steps, and heard a fall, after which he ran up and found Marjory.

'I sent her into the schoolroom to bring my paper-knife,' said the Doctor; 'if I had but gone myself—! But why should she have gone outside on a frosty night like this?'

'Oh, Dr. Dering!' I broke out, 'I'm afraid—I'm afraid she went for me!'

I saw Ormsby's face as I spoke, and there was a look upon it which made me pity him.

'And you sent my poor child out on your errand, Cameron! Could you not have done it yourself?'

'I wish I had!' I exclaimed; 'oh, I wish I had! I tried to stop her, and then—and then it was too late. Please tell me, sir, is she badly hurt?'

'How can I tell?' he said harshly; 'there, I can't speak of this just yet: go, both of you.'

There was little work done at evening preparation that night; the whole school was buzzing with curiosity and speculation, as we heard doors opening and shutting around, and the wheels of the doctor's gig as it rolled up the chestnut avenue.

I sat with my hands shielding my eyes and ears, engaged to all appearance with the books before me, while my restless thoughts were employed in making earnest resolutions for the future.

At last I saw my cowardice in its true light, and felt impatient to tell Marjory that I did so, to prove to her that I had really reformed; but when would an opportunity come? I might not see her again for days, perhaps not at all till after the holidays; but I would not let myself dwell upon such a contingency as that, and, to banish it, tried to picture what Marjory would say, and how she would look, when I was allowed to see her again.

After evening prayers, read by one of the assistant-masters, for the Doctor did not appear again, we were enjoined to go up to our bedrooms with as little noise as possible, and we had been in bed some time before Sutcliffe, the old butler, came up as usual to put out the lights.

On this occasion he was assailed by a fire of eager whispers from every door: 'Sutcliffe, hi! old Sutty, how is she?' but he did not seem to hear, until a cry louder than the rest brought him to our room.

'For God's sake, gentlemen, don't!' he said, in a hoarse whisper, as he turned out the light; 'they'll hear you downstairs.'

'But how is she? do you know—better?'

'Ay,' he said, 'she's better. She'll be over her trouble soon, will Miss Marjory!'

A low murmur of delight ran round the room, which the butler tried to check in vain.

'Don't!' he said again, 'wait—wait till morning.... Go to sleep quiet now, and I'll come up first thing and tell you.'

He had no sooner turned his back than the general relief broke out irrepressibly; Ormsby being especially demonstrative. 'Didn't I tell you fellows so?' he said triumphantly; 'as if it was likely a plucky girl like Marjory would mind a little cut like that. She'll be all right in the morning, you see!'

But this confidence jarred upon me, who could not pretend to share it, until I was unable to restrain the torturing anxiety I felt.

'You're wrong—all of you!' I cried, 'I'm sure she's not better. Didn't you hear how Sutcliffe said it? She's worse—she may even be dying!'

I met with the usual treatment of a prophet of evil. 'You young muff,' I was told on all sides, 'who asked your opinion? Who are you, to know better than anyone else?'

Ormsby attacked me hotly for trying to excite a groundless alarm, and I was recommended to hold my tongue and go to sleep.

I said no more, but I could not sleep; the others dropped off one by one, Ormsby being the last; but I lay awake listening and thinking, until the dread and suspense grew past bearing. I must know the truth. I would go down and find the Doctor, and beg him to tell me; he might be angry and punish me—but that would be nothing in comparison with the relief of knowing my fear was unfounded.

Stealthily I slipped out of bed, stole through the dim room to the door, and down the old staircase, which creaked under my bare feet. The dog in the yard howled as I passed the big window, through which the stars were sparkling frostily in the keen blue sky. Outside the room in which Marjory lay, I listened, but could hear nothing. At least she was sleeping, then, and, relieved already, I went on down to the hall.

The big clock on a table there was ticking solemnly, like a slow footfall; the lamp was alight, so the Doctor must be still up. With a heart that beat loudly I went to his study door and lifted my hand to knock, when from within rose a sound at which the current of my blood stopped and ran backwards—the terrible, heartbroken grief of a grown man.

Boy as I was, I felt that an agony like that was sacred; besides, I knew the worst then.

I dragged myself upstairs again, cold to the bones, with a brain that was frozen too. My one desire was to reach my bed, cover my face, and let the tears flow; though, when I did regain it, no tears and no thoughts came. I lay there and shivered for some time, with a stony, stunned sensation, and then I slept—as if Marjory were well.

The next morning the bell under the cupola did not clang, and Sutcliffe came up with the direction that we were to go down very quietly, and not to draw up the window-blinds; and then we all knew what had happened during the night.

There was a very genuine grief, though none knew Marjory as I had known her; the more emotional wept, the older ones indulged in little semi-pious conventional comments, oddly foreign to their usual tone; all—even the most thoughtless—felt the same hush and awe overtake them.

I could not cry; I felt nothing, except a dull rage at my own insensibility. Marjory was dead—and I had no tears.

Morning school was a mere pretence that day; we dreaded, for almost the first time, to see the Doctor's face, but he did not show himself, and the arrangements necessary for the breaking-up of the school were made by the matron.

Some, including Ormsby and myself, could not be taken in for some days, during which we had to remain at the school: days of shadow and monotony, with occasional ghastly outbreaks of the high spirits which nothing could repress, even in that house of mourning.

But the time passed at last, until it was the evening of the day on which Marjory had been left to her last sleep.

The poor father and mother had been unable to stay in the house now that it no longer covered even what had been their child; and the only two, besides the matron and a couple of servants who still remained there, were Ormsby and I, who were both to leave on the following morning.

I would rather have been alone just then with anyone but Ormsby, though he had never since that fatal night taken the slightest notice of me; he looked worn and haggard to a degree that made me sure he must have cared more for Marjory than I could have imagined, and yet he would break at times into a feverish gaiety which surprised and repelled me.

He was in one of these latter moods that evening, as we sat, as far apart as possible, in the empty, firelit schoolroom.

'Now, Cameron,' he said, as he came up to me and struck me boisterously on the shoulder, 'wake up, man! I've been in the blues long enough. We can't go on moping always, on the night before the holidays, too! Do something to make yourself sociable—talk, can't you?'

'No, I can't,' I said; and, breaking from him, went to one of the windows and looked vacantly out into blackness, which reflected the long room, with its dingy greenish maps, and the desks and forms glistening in the fire-beams.

The ice-bound state in which I had been so long was slowly passing away, now that the scene by the little grave that raw, cheerless morning had brought home remorselessly the truth that Marjory was indeed gone—lost to me for ever.

I could see now what she had been to me; how she had made my great loneliness endurable; how, with her innocent, fearless nature, she had tried to rouse me from spiritless and unmanly dejection. And I could never hope to please her now by proving that I had learnt the lesson; she had gone from me to some world infinitely removed, in which I was forgotten, and my pitiful trials and struggles could be nothing to her any more!

I was once more alone, and this second bereavement revived in all its crushing desolation the first bitter loss which it so closely followed.

So, as I stood there at the window, my unnatural calm could hold out no longer; the long-frozen tears thawed, and I could weep for the first time since Marjory died.

But I was not allowed to sorrow undisturbed; I felt a rough grasp on my arm, as Ormsby asked me angrily, 'What's the matter now?'

'Oh, Marjory, come to me!' I could only cry; 'I can't bear it! I can't! I can't!'

'Stop that, do you hear?' he said savagely, 'I won't have it! Who are you to cry about her, when—but for you—'

He got no farther; the bitter truth in such a taunt, coming from him, stung me to ungovernable rage. I turned and struck him full in the mouth, which I cut open with my clenched hand.

His eyes became all pupil. 'You shall pay me for that!' he said through his teeth; and, forcing me against a desk, he caught up a large T-square which lay near; he was far the stronger, and I felt myself powerless in his grasp. Passion and pain had made him beside himself for the moment, and he did not know how formidable a weapon the heavily-weighted instrument might become in his hand.

I shut my eyes: I think I rather hoped he would kill me, and then perhaps I might go where Marjory was. I did not cry for help, and it would have been useless if I had done so, for the schoolroom was a long way from the kitchen and offices of that rambling old house.

But before the expected blow was dealt I felt his grasp relax, and heard the instrument fall with a sudden clatter on the floor. 'Look,' he whispered, in a voice I did not recognise, 'look there!'

And when I opened my eyes, I saw Marjory standing between us!

She looked just as I had always seen her: I suppose that even the after-life could not make Marjory look purer, or more lovely than she was on earth. My first feeling was a wild conviction that it had all been some strange mistake—that Marjory was not dead.

'Marjory, Marjory!' I cried in my joy, 'is it really you? You have come back, after all, and it is not true!'

She looked at us both without speaking for a moment; her dear brown eyes had lost their old childish sparkle, and were calm and serious as if with a deeper knowledge.

Ormsby had cowered back to the opposite wall, covering his face. 'Go away!' he gasped. 'Cameron—you ask her to go. She—she liked you.... I never meant it. Tell her I never meant to do it!'

I could not understand such terror at the sight of Marjory, even if she had been what he thought her; but there was a reason in his case.

'You were going to hurt Cameron,' said Marjory, at length, and her voice sounded sad and grave and far-away.

'I don't care, Marjory,' I cried, 'not now you are here!'

She motioned me back: 'You must not come nearer,' she said. 'I cannot stay long, and I must speak to Ormsby. Ormsby, have you told anyone?'

'No,' he said, shaking all over, 'it could do no good.... I thought I needn't.'

'Tell him,' said Marjory.

'Must I? Oh, no, no!' he groaned, 'don't make me do that!'

'You must,' she answered, and he turned to me with a sullen fear.

'It was like this,' he began; 'that night, when I was waiting for you down there—I had some string, and it struck me, all in a moment, that it would be fun to trip you up. I didn't mean to hurt you—only frighten you. I fastened the string across a little way from the bottom. And then'—he had to moisten his lips before he could go on—'then she came down, and I tried to catch her—and couldn't—no, I couldn't!'

'Is that all?' asked Marjory, as he stopped short.

'I cut the string and hid it before you came. Now you know, and you may tell if you like!'

'Cameron, you will never tell, will you—as long as he lives?' said Marjory. 'You must promise.'

I was horrified by what I had heard; but her eyes were upon me, and I promised.

'And you, Ormsby, promise me to be kinder to him after this.'

He could not speak; but he made a sign of assent.

'And now,' said Marjory, 'shake hands with him and forgive him.'

But I revolted: 'No, Marjory, I can't; not now—when I know this!'

'Cameron, dear,' she said, 'you won't let me go away sorry, will you? and I must go so soon. For my sake, when I wish it so!'

I went to Ormsby, and took his cold, passive hand. 'I do forgive him, Marjory,' I said.

She smiled brightly at us both. 'And you won't forget, either of you?' she said. 'And, Douglas, you will be brave, and take your own part now. Good-bye, good-bye.'

I tried to reach her. 'Don't leave me; take me with you, Marjory—dear, dear Marjory, don't go!' But there was only firelit space where she had stood, though the sound of her pleading, pathetic voice was still in the air.

Ormsby remained for a few minutes leaning against a desk, with his face buried in his arms, and I heard him struggling with his sobs. At last he rose, and left the room without a word.

But I stayed there where I had last seen Marjory, till the fire died down, and the hour was late, for I was glad to be alone with the new and solemn joy that had come to me. For she had not forgotten me where she was; I had been allowed to see her once more, and it might even be that I should see her again. And I resolved then that when she came she should find me more worthy of her.

From that night my character seemed to enter upon a new phase, and when I returned to school it was to begin my second term under better auspices.

My cousins had welcomed me cordially among them, and as I mastered the lesson of give and take, of respecting one's self in respecting others, which I needed to learn, my early difficulties vanished with the weakness that had produced them.

By Ormsby I was never again molested; in word and deed, he was true to the promise exacted from him during that last strange scene. At first, he avoided me as being too painfully connected with the past; but by degrees, as he recognised that his secret was safe in my keeping, we grew to understand one another better, although it would be too much to say that we ever became intimate.

After he went to Sandhurst I lost sight of him, and only a few months since the news of his death in the Soudan, where he fell gallantly, made me sorrowfully aware that we should never meet again.

I had a lingering fancy that Marjory might appear to me once more, but I have long since given up all hope of that in this life, and for what may come after I am content to wait.

But the charge my child-friend had undertaken was completed on the night she was allowed to return to earth and determine the crisis of two lives; there is nothing now to call the bright and gracious little spirit back, for her influence will remain always.

The Good Little Girl

Her name was Priscilla Prodgers, and she was a very good little girl indeed. So good was she, in fact, that she could not help being aware of it herself, and that is a stage to which very many quite excellent persons never succeed in attaining. She was only just a child, it is true, but she had read a great many beautiful story-books, and so she knew what a powerful reforming influence a childish and innocent remark, or a youthful example, or a happy combination of both, can exert over grown-up people. And early in life—she was but eleven at the date of this history—early in life she had seen clearly that her mission was to reform her family and relatives generally. This was a heavy task for one so young, particularly in Priscilla's case, for, besides a father, mother, brother, and sister, in whom she could not but discern many and serious failings, she possessed an aunt who was addicted to insincerity, two female cousins whose selfishness and unamiability were painful to witness, and a male cousin who talked slang and was so worldly that he habitually went about in yellow boots! Nevertheless Priscilla did not flinch, although, for some reason, her earnest and unremitting efforts had hitherto failed to produce any deep impression. At times she thought this was owing to the fact that she tried to reform all her family together, and that her best plan would be to take each one separately, and devote her whole energies to improving that person alone. But then she never could make up her mind which member of the family to begin with. It is small wonder that she often felt a little disheartened, but even that was a cheering symptom, for in the books it is generally just when the little heroine becomes most discouraged that the seemingly impenitent relative exhibits the first sign of softening.

So Priscilla persevered: sometimes with merely a shocked glance of disapproval, which she had practised before the looking-glass until she could do it perfectly; sometimes with some tender, tactful little hint. 'Don't you think, dear papa,' she would say softly, on a Sunday morning, 'don't you think you could write your newspaper article on some other day—is it a work of real necessity?' Or she would ask her mother, who was certainly fond of wearing pretty things. 'How much bread for poor starving people would the price of your new bonnet buy, mother? I should so like to work it out on my little slate!'

Then she would remind her brother Alick that it would be so much better if, instead of wasting his time in playing with silly little tin soldiers, he would try to learn as much as he could before he was sent to school; while she was never tired of quoting to her sister Betty the line, 'Be good, sweet maid, and let who will be clever!' which Betty, quite unjustly, interpreted to mean that Priscilla thought but poorly of her sister's intellectual capacity. Once when, as a great treat, the children were allowed to read 'Ivanhoe' aloud, Priscilla declined to participate until she had conscientiously read up the whole Norman period in her English history; and on another occasion she cried bitterly on hearing that her mother had arranged for them to learn dancing, and even endured bread and water for an entire day rather than consent to acquire an accomplishment which she feared, from what she had read, would prove a snare. On the second day—well, there was roast beef and Yorkshire pudding for dinner, and Priscilla yielded; but she made the resolution—and kept it too—that, if she went to the dancing class, she would firmly refuse to take the slightest pains to learn a single step.

I only mention all these traits to show that Priscilla really was an unusually good child, which makes it the more sad and strange that her family should have profited so little by her example. She was neither loved nor respected as she ought to have been, I am grieved to say. Her papa, when he was not angry, made the cruellest fun of her mild reproofs; her mother continued to spend money on dresses and bonnets, and even allowed the maid to say that her mistress was 'not at home,' when she was merely unwilling to receive visitors. Alick and Betty, too, only grew more exasperated when Priscilla urged them to keep their tempers, and altogether she could not help feeling how wasted and thrown away she was in such a circle.

But she never quite lost heart; her papa was a literary man and wrote tales, some of which she feared were not as true as they affected to be, while he invariably neglected to insert a moral in any of them; frequently she dropped little remarks before him with apparent carelessness, in the hope that he might put them in print—but he never did; she never could recognise herself as a character in any of his stories, and so at last she gave up reading them at all!

But one morning she came more near to giving up in utter despair than ever before. Only the previous day she had been so hopeful! her father had really seemed to be beginning to appreciate his little daughter, and had presented her with sixpence in the new coinage to put in her money-box. This had emboldened her to such a degree that, happening on the following morning to hear him ejaculate 'Confound it!' she had, pressing one hand to her beating heart and laying the other hand softly upon his shoulder (which is the proper attitude on these occasions), reminded him that such an expression was scarcely less reprehensible than actual bad language. Upon which her hard-hearted papa had told her, almost sharply, 'not to be a little prig!'

Priscilla forgave him, of course, and freely, because he was her father and it was her duty to bear with him; but she felt the injustice deeply, for all that. Then, when she went up into the nursery, Alick and Betty made a frantic uproar, merely because she insisted on teaching them the moves in chess, when they perversely wanted to play Halma! So, feeling baffled and sick at heart, she had put on her hat and run out all alone to a quiet lane near her home, where she could soothe her troubled mind by thinking over the ingratitude and lack of appreciation with which her efforts were met.

She had not gone very far up the lane when she saw, seated on a bench, a bent old woman in a poke-bonnet with a crutch-handled stick in her hands, and this old woman Priscilla (who was very quick of observation) instantly guessed to be a fairy—in which, as it fell out, she was perfectly right.

'Good day, my pretty child!' croaked the old dame.

'Good-day to you, ma'am!' answered Priscilla politely (for she knew that it was not only right but prudent to be civil to fairies, particularly when they take the form of old women). 'But, if you please, you mustn't call me pretty—because I am not. At least,' she added, for she prided herself upon her truthfulness, 'not exactly pretty. And I should hate to be always thinking about my looks, like poor Milly—she's our housemaid, you know—and I so often have to tell her that she did not make her own face.'

'I don't alarm you, I see,' said the old crone; 'but possibly you're not aware that you're talking to a fairy?'

'Oh, yes, I am—but I'm not a bit afraid, because, you see, fairies can only hurt bad children.'

'Ah, and you're a good little child—that's not difficult to see!'

'They don't see it at home!' said Priscilla, with a sad little sigh, 'or they would listen more when I tell them of things they oughtn't to do.'

'And what things do they do that they oughtn't to, my child—if you don't mind telling me?'

'Oh, I don't mind in the least!' Priscilla hastened to assure her; and then she told the old woman all her family's faults, and the trial it was to bear with them and go on trying to induce them to mend their ways. 'And papa is getting worse than ever,' she concluded dolefully; 'only fancy, this very morning he called me a little prig!'

'Tut, tut!' said the fairy sympathetically, 'deary, deary me! So he called you that, did he?—"a little prig"! And you, too! Ah, the world's coming to a pretty pass! I suppose, now, your papa and the rest of them have got it into their heads that you are too young and too inexperienced to set up as their adviser—is that it?'

'I'm afraid so,' admitted Priscilla; 'but we mustn't blame them,' she added gently, 'we must remember that they don't know any better—mustn't we, ma'am?'

'You sweet child!' said the old lady with enthusiasm; 'I must see if I can't do something to help you, though I'm not the fairy I used to be—still, there are tricks I can manage still, if I'm put to it. What you want is something that will prove to them that they ought to pay more attention to you, eh?—something there can be no possible mistake about?'

'Yes!' cried Priscilla eagerly, 'and—and—how would it be if you changed them into something else, just to show them, and then I could ask for them to be transformed back again, you know?'

'What an ingenious little thing you are!' exclaimed the fairy; 'but, let us see—if you came home and found your cruel papa doing duty as the family hatstand, or strutting about as a Cochin China fowl—'

'Oh, yes; and I'd feed him every day, till he was sorry!' interrupted the warmhearted little girl impulsively.

'Ah, but you're so hasty, my dear. Who would write all the clever articles and tales to earn bread and meat for you all?—fowls can't use a pen. No, we must find a prettier trick than that—there was one I seem to remember, long, long ago, performing for a good little ill-used girl, just like you, my dearie, just like you! Now what was it? some gift I gave her whenever she opened her lips—'

'Why, I remember—how funny that you should have forgotten! Whenever she opened her lips, roses, and diamonds, and rubies fell out. That would be the very thing! Then they'd have to attend to me! Oh, do be a kind old fairy and give me a gift like that—do, do!'

'Now, don't be so impetuous! You forget that this is not the time of year for roses, and, as for jewels, well, I don't think I can be very far wrong in supposing that you open your lips pretty frequently in the course of the day?'

'Alick does call me a "mag,"' said Priscilla; 'but that's wrong, because I never speak without having something to say. I don't think people ought to—it may do so much harm; mayn't it?'

'Undoubtedly. But, anyhow, if we made it every time you opened your lips, you would soon ruin me in precious stones, that's plain! No, I think we had better say that the jewels shall only drop when you are saying something you wish to be particularly improving—how will that do?'

'Very nicely indeed, ma'am, thank you,' said Priscilla, 'because, you see, it comes to just the same thing.'

'Ah, well, try to be as economical of your good things as you can—remember that in these hard times a poor old fairy's riches are not as inexhaustible as they used to be.'

'And jewels really will drop out?'

'Whenever they are wanted to "point a moral and adorn a tale,"' said the old woman (who, for a fairy, was particularly well-read). 'There, run along home, do, and scatter your pearls before your relations.'

It need scarcely be said that Priscilla was only too willing to obey; she ran all the way home with a light heart, eager to exhibit her wonderful gift. 'How surprised they will be!' she was thinking. 'If it had been Betty, instead of me, I suppose she would have come back talking toads! It would have been a good lesson for her—but still, toads are nasty things, and it would have been rather unpleasant for the rest of us. I think I won't tell Betty where I met the fairy.'

She came in and took her place demurely at the family luncheon, which was the children's dinner; they were all seated already, including her father, who had got through most of his writing in the course of the morning.

'Now make haste and eat your dinner, Priscilla,' said her mother, 'or it will be quite cold.'

'I always let it get a little cold, mother,' replied the good little girl, 'so that I mayn't come to think too much about eating, you know.'

As she uttered this remark, she felt a jewel producing itself in some mysterious way from the tip of her tongue, and saw it fall with a clatter into her plate. 'I'll pretend not to notice anything,' she thought.

'Hullo!' exclaimed Alick, pausing in the act of mastication, 'I say—Prissie!'

'If you ask mother, I'm sure she will tell you that it is most ill-mannered to speak with your mouth full,' said Priscilla, her speech greatly impeded by an immense emerald.

'I like that!' exclaimed her rude brother; 'who's speaking with their mouth full now?'

'"Their" is not grammar, dear,' was Priscilla's only reply to this taunt, as she delicately ejected a pearl, 'you should say her mouth full.' For Priscilla's grammar was as good as her principles.

'But really, Priscilla, dear,' said her mother, who felt some embarrassment at so novel an experience as being obliged to find fault with her little daughter, 'you should not eat sweets just before dinner, and—and couldn't you get rid of them in some other manner?'

'Sweets!' cried Priscilla, considerably annoyed at being so misunderstood, 'they are not sweets, mother. Look!' And she offered to submit one for inspection.

'If I may venture to express an opinion,' observed her father, 'I would rather that a child of mine should suck sweets than coloured beads, and in either case I object to having them prominently forced upon my notice at meal-times. But I daresay I'm wrong. I generally am.'

'Papa is quite right, dear,' said her mother, 'it is such a dangerous habit—suppose you were to swallow one, you know! Put them in the fire, like a good girl, and go on with your dinner.'

Priscilla rose without a word, her cheeks crimsoning, and dropped the pearl, ruby, and emerald, with great accuracy, into the very centre of the fire. This done, she returned to her seat, and went on with her dinner in silence, though her feelings prevented her from eating very much.

'If they choose to think my pearls are only beads, or jujubes, or acidulated drops,' she said to herself, bitterly, 'I won't waste any more on them, that's all! I won't open my lips again, except to say quite ordinary things—so there!'

If Priscilla had not been such a very good little girl, you might almost have thought she was in a temper; but she was not; her feelings were wounded, that was all, which is quite a different thing.

That afternoon, her aunt Margarine, Mrs. Hoyle, came to call. She was the aunt whom we have already mentioned as being given to insincerity; she was not well off, and had a tendency to flatter people; but Priscilla was fond of her notwithstanding, and she had never detected her in any insincerity towards herself. She was sent into the drawing-room to entertain her aunt until her mother was ready to come down, and her aunt, as usual, overwhelmed her with affectionate admiration. 'How pretty and well you are looking, my pet!' she began, 'and oh, what a beautiful frock you have on!'

'The little silkworms wore it before I did, aunt,' said Priscilla, modestly.

'How sweet of you to say so! But they never looked half so well in it, I'll be bou—Why, my child, you've dropped a stone out of a brooch or something. Look—on the carpet there!'

'Oh,' said Priscilla, carelessly, 'it was out of my mouth—not out of a brooch, I never wear jewellery. I think jewellery makes people grow so conceited; don't you, Aunt Margarine?'

'Yes, indeed, dearest—indeed you are so right!' said her aunt (who wore a cameo-brooch as large as a tart upon her cloak), 'and—and surely that can't be a diamond in your lap?'

'Oh, yes, it is. I met a fairy this morning in the lane, and so—' and here Priscilla proceeded to narrate her wonderful experience. 'I thought it might perhaps make papa and mamma value me a little more than they do,' she said wistfully, as she finished her story, 'but they don't take the least notice; they made me put the jewels on the fire—they did, really!'

'What blindness!' cried her aunt; 'how can people shut their eyes to such a treasure? And—and may I just have one look? What, you really don't want them?—I may keep them for my very own? You precious love! Ah, I know a humble home where you would be appreciated at your proper worth. What would I not give for my poor naughty Belle and Cathie to have the advantage of seeing more of such a cousin!'

'I don't know whether I could do them much good,' said Priscilla, 'but I would try my best.'

'I am sure you would!' said Aunt Margarine, 'and now, dearest sweet, I am going to ask your dear mamma to spare you to us for just a little while; we must both beg very hard.'

'I'll go and tell nurse to pack my things now, and then I can go away with you,' said the little girl.

When her mother heard of the invitation, she consented quite willingly. 'To tell you the truth, Margarine,' she said, 'I shall be very glad for the child to have a change. She seems a little unhappy at home with us, and she behaved most unlike her usual self at lunch; it can't be natural for a child of her age to chew large glass beads. Did your Cathie and Belle ever do such a thing?'

'Never,' said Aunt Margarine, coughing. 'It is a habit that certainly ought to be checked, and I promise you, my dear Lucy, that if you will only trust Priscilla to me, I will take away anything of that kind the very moment I find it. And I do think, poor as we are, we shall manage to make her feel at home. We are all so fond of your sweet Priscilla!'

So the end of it was that Priscilla went to stay with her aunt that very afternoon, and her family bore the parting with the greatest composure.

'I can't give you nice food, or a pretty bedroom to sleep in such as you have at home,' said her kind aunt. 'We are very plain people, my pet; but at least we can promise you a warm welcome.'

'Oh, auntie,' protested Priscilla, 'you mustn't think I mind a little hardship! Why, if beds weren't hard and food not nicely cooked now and then, we should soon grow too luxurious to do our duty, and that would be so very bad for us!'

'Oh, what beauties!' cried her aunt, involuntarily, as she stooped to recover several sparkling gems from the floor of the cab. 'I mean—it's better to pick them up, dear, don't you think? they might get in people's way, you know. What a blessing you will be in our simple home! I want you to do all you can to instruct your cousins; don't be afraid of telling them of any faults you may happen to see. Poor Cathie and Belle, I fear they are very far from being all they should be!' and Aunt Margarine heaved a sigh.

'Never mind, auntie; they will be better in time, I am sure. I wasn't always a good girl.'

Priscilla thoroughly enjoyed the first few days of her visit; even her aunt was only too grateful for instruction, and begged that Priscilla would tell her, quite candidly, of any shortcomings she might notice. And Priscilla, very kindly and considerately, always did tell her. Belle and Catherine were less docile, and she saw that it would take her some time to win their esteem and affection; but this was just what Priscilla liked: it was the usual experience of the heroines in the books, and much more interesting, too, than conquering her cousins' hearts at once.

Still, both Catherine and Belle persistently hardened their hearts against their gentle little cousin in the unkindest way; they would scarcely speak to her, and chose to make a grievance out of the fact that one or other of them was obliged, by their mother's strict orders, to be constantly in attendance upon her, in order to pick up and bring Mrs. Hoyle all the jewels that Priscilla scattered in profusion wherever she went.

'If you would only carry a plate about with you, Priscilla,' complained Belle one day, 'you could catch the jewels in that.'

'But I don't want to catch the jewels, dear Belle,' said Priscilla, with a playful but very sweet smile; 'if other people prize such things, that is not my fault, is it? Jewels do not make people any happier, Belle!'

'I should think not!' exclaimed Belle. 'I'm sure my back perfectly aches with stooping, and so does Cathie's. There! that big topaz has just gone and rolled under the sideboard, and mother will be so angry if I don't get it out! It is too bad of you, Priscilla! I believe you do it on purpose!'

'Ah, you will know me better some day, dear, was the gentle response.

'Well, at all events, I think you might be naughty just now and then, Prissie, and give Cathie and me a half-holiday.'

'I would do anything else to please you, dear, but not that; you must not ask me to do what is impossible.'

Alas! not even this angelic behaviour, not even the loving admonitions, the tender rebukes, the shocked reproaches that fell, accompanied by perfect cascades of jewels, from the lips of our pattern little Priscilla, succeeded in removing the utterly unfounded prejudices of her cousins, though it was some consolation to feel that she was gradually acquiring a most beneficial influence over her aunt, who called Priscilla 'her little conscience.' For, you see, Priscilla's conscience had so little to do on her own account that it was always at the service of other people, and indeed quite enjoyed being useful, as was only natural to a conscientious conscience which felt that it could never have been created to be idle.

Very soon another responsibility was added to little Priscilla's burdens. Her cousin Dick, the worldly one with the yellow boots, came home after his annual holiday, which, as he was the junior clerk in a large bank, he was obliged to take rather late in the year. She had looked forward to his return with some excitement. Dick, she knew, was frivolous and reckless in his habits—he went to the theatre occasionally and frequently spent an evening in playing billiards and smoking cigars at a friend's house. There would be real credit in reforming poor cousin Dick.

He was not long, of course, in hearing of Priscilla's marvellous endowment, and upon the first occasion they were alone together treated her with a respect and admiration which he had very certainly never shown her before.

'You're wonderful, Prissie!' he said; 'I'd no idea you had it in you!'

'Nor had I, Dick; but it shows that even a little girl can do something.'

'I should rather think so! and—and the way you look—as grave as a judge all the time! Prissie, I wish you'd tell me how you manage it, I wouldn't tell a soul.'

'But I don't know, Dick. I only talk and the jewels come—that is all.'

'You artful little girl! you can keep a secret, I see, but so can I. And you might tell me how you do the trick. What put you up to the dodge? I'm to be trusted, I assure you.'

'Dick, you can't—you mustn't—think there is any trickery about it! How can you believe I could be such a wicked little girl as to play tricks? It was an old fairy that gave me the gift. I'm sure I don't know why—unless she thought that I was a good child and deserved to be encouraged.'

'By Jove!' cried Dick, 'I never knew you were half such fun!'

'I am not fun, Dick. I think fun is generally so very vulgar, and oh, I wish you wouldn't say "by Jove!" Surely you know he was a heathen god!'

'I seem to have heard of him in some such capacity,' said Dick. 'I say, Prissie, what a ripping big ruby!'

'Ah, Dick, Dick, you are like the others! I'm afraid you think more of the jewels than of any words I may say—and yet jewels are common enough!'

'They seem to be with you. Pearls, too, and such fine ones! Here, Priscilla, take them; they're your property.'

Priscilla put her hands behind her: 'No, indeed, Dick, they are of no use to me. Keep them, please; they may help to remind you of what I have said.'

'It's awfully kind of you,' said Dick, looking really touched. 'Then—since you put it in that way—thanks, I will, Priscilla. I'll have them made into a horse-shoe pin.'

'You mustn't let it make you too fond of dress, then,' said Priscilla; 'but I'm afraid you're that already, Dick.'

'A diamond!' he cried; 'go on, Priscilla, I'm listening—pitch into me, it will do me a lot of good!'

But Priscilla thought it wisest to say no more just then.

That night, after Priscilla and Cathie and Belle had gone to bed, Dick and his mother sat up talking until a late hour.

'Is dear little cousin Priscilla to be a permanency in this establishment?' began her cousin, stifling a yawn, for there had been a rather copious flow of precious stones during the evening.

'Well, I shall keep her with us as long as I can,' said Mrs. Hoyle, 'she's such a darling, and they don't seem to want her at home. I'm sure, limited as my means are, I'm most happy to have such a visitor.'

'She seems to pay her way—only her way is a trifle trying at times, isn't it? She lectured me for half an hour on end without a single check!'

'Are you sure you picked them all up, dear boy?'

'Got a few of the best in my waistcoat-pocket now. I'm afraid I scrunched a pearl or two, though: they were all over the place, you know. I suppose you've been collecting too, mater?'

'I picked up one or two,' said his mother; 'I should think I must have nearly enough now to fill a bandbox. And that brings me to what I wanted to consult you about, Richard. How are we to dispose of them? She has given them all to me.'

'You haven't done anything with them yet, then?'

'How could I? I have been obliged to stay at home: I've been so afraid of letting that precious child go out of my sight for a single hour, for fear some unscrupulous persons might get hold of her. I thought that perhaps, when you came home, you would dispose of the jewels for me.'

'But, mater,' protested Dick, 'I can't go about asking who'll buy a whole bandbox full of jewels!'

'Oh, very well, then; I suppose we must go on living this hugger-mugger life when we have the means of being as rich as princes, just because you are too lazy and selfish to take a little trouble!'

'I know something about these things,' said Dick. 'I know a fellow who's a diamond merchant, and it's not so easy to sell a lot of valuable stones as you seem to imagine, mother. And then Priscilla really overdoes it, you know—why, if she goes on like this, she'll make diamonds as cheap as currants!'

'I should have thought that was a reason for selling them as soon as possible; but I'm only a woman, and of course my opinion is worth nothing! Still, you might take some of the biggest to your friend, and accept whatever he'll give you for them—there are plenty more, you needn't haggle over the price.'

'He'd want to know all about them, and what should I say? I can't tell him a cousin of mine produces them whenever she feels disposed.'

'You could say they have been in the family for some time, and you are obliged to part with them; I don't ask you to tell a falsehood, Richard.'

'Well, to tell you the honest truth,' said Dick, 'I'd rather have nothing to do with it. I'm not proud, but I shouldn't like it to get about among our fellows at the bank that I went about hawking diamonds.'

'But, you stupid, undutiful boy, don't you see that you could leave the bank—you need never do anything any more—we should all live rich and happy somewhere in the country, if we could only sell those jewels! And you won't do that one little thing!'

'Well,' said Dick, 'I'll think over it. I'll see what I can do.'

And his mother knew that it was perfectly useless to urge him any further: for, in some things, Dick was as obstinate as a mule, and, in others, far too easy-going and careless ever to succeed in life. He had promised to think over it, however, and she had to be contented with that.

On the evening following this conversation cousin Dick entered the sitting-room the moment after his return from the City, and found his mother to all appearances alone.

'What a dear sweet little guileless angel cousin Priscilla is, to be sure!' was his first remark.

'Then you have sold some of the stones!' cried Aunt Margarine. 'Sit down, like a good boy, and tell me all about it.'

'Well,' said Dick, 'I took the finest diamonds and rubies and pearls that escaped from that saintlike child last night in the course of some extremely disparaging comments on my character and pursuits—I took those jewels to Faycett and Rosewater's in New Bond Street—you know the shop, on the right-hand side as you go up—'

'Oh, go on, Dick; go on—never mind where it is—how much did you get for them?'

'I'm coming to that; keep cool, dear mamma. Well, I went in, and I saw the manager, and I said: "I want you to make these up into a horse-shoe scarf-pin for me."'

'You said that! You never tried to sell one? Oh, Dick, you are too provoking!'

'Hold on, mater; I haven't done yet. So the manager—a very gentlemanly person, rather thin on the top of the head—not that that affects his business capacities; for, after all—'

'Dick, do you want to drive me frantic!'

'I can't conceive any domestic occurrence which would be more distressing or generally inconvenient, mother dear. You do interrupt a fellow so! I forgot where I was now—oh, the manager, ah yes! Well, the manager said, "We shall be very happy to have the stones made in any design you may select"— jewellery, by the way, seems to exercise a most refining influence upon the manners: this man had the deportment of a duke—"you may select," he said; "but of course I need not tell you that none of these stones are genuine."'

'Not genuine!' cried Aunt Margarine excitedly. 'They must be—he was lying!'

'West-end jewellers never lie,' said Dick; 'but naturally, when he said that, I told him I should like to have some proof of his assertion. "Will you take the risk of testing?" said he. "Test away, my dear man!" said I. So he brought a little wheel near the emerald—"whizz!" and away went the emerald! Then he let a drop of something fall on the ruby—and it fizzled up for all the world like pink champagne. "Go on, don't mind me!" I told him, so he touched the diamond with an electric wire—"phit!" and there was only something that looked like the ash of a shocking bad cigar. Then the pearls—and they popped like so many air-balloons. "Are you satisfied?" he asked.

'"Oh, perfectly,"' said I, '"you needn't trouble about the horse-shoe pin now. Good evening," and so I came away, after thanking him for his very amusing scientific experiments.'

'And do you believe that the jewels are all shams, Dick?—do you really?'

'I think it so probable that nothing on earth will induce me to offer a single one for sale. I should never hear the last of it at the bank. No, mater, dear little Priscilla's sparkling conversation may be unspeakably precious from a moral point of view, but it has no commercial value. Those jewels are bogus—shams every stone of them!'

Now, all this time our heroine had been sitting unperceived in a corner behind a window-curtain, reading 'The Wide, Wide World,' a work which she was never weary of perusing. Some children would have come forward earlier, but Priscilla was never a forward child, and she remained as quiet as a little mouse up to the moment when she could control her feelings no longer.

'It isn't true!' she cried passionately, bursting out of her retreat and confronting her cousin; 'it's cruel and unkind to say my jewels are shams! They are real—they are, they are!'

'Hullo, Prissie!' said her abandoned cousin; 'so you combine jewel-dropping with eaves-dropping, eh?'

'How dare you!' cried Aunt Margarine, almost beside herself, 'you odious little prying minx, setting up to teach your elders and your betters with your cut and dried priggish maxims! When I think how I have petted and indulged you all this time, and borne with the abominable litter you left in every room you entered—and now to find you are only a little, conceited, hypocritical impostor—oh, why haven't I words to express my contempt for such conduct—why am I dumb at such a moment as this?'

'Come, mother,' said her son soothingly, 'that's not such a bad beginning; I should call it fairly fluent and expressive, myself.'

'Be quiet, Dick! I'm speaking to this wicked child, who has obtained our love and sympathy and attention on false pretences, for which she ought to be put in prison—yes, in prison, for such a heartless trick on relatives who can ill afford to be so cruelly disappointed!'

'But, aunt!' expostulated poor Priscilla, 'you always said you only kept the jewels as souvenirs, and that it did you so much good to hear me talk!'

'Don't argue with me, miss! If I had known the stones were wretched tawdry imitations, do you imagine for an instant—?'

'Now, mother,' said Dick, 'be fair—they were uncommonly good imitations, you must admit that!'

'Indeed, indeed I thought they were real, the fairy never told me!'

'After all,' said Dick, 'it's not Priscilla's fault. She can't help it if the stones aren't real, and she made up for quality by quantity anyhow; didn't you, Prissie?'

'Hold your tongue, Richard; she could help it, she knew it all the time, and she's a hateful, sanctimonious little stuck-up viper, and so I tell her to her face!'

Priscilla could scarcely believe that kind, indulgent, smooth-spoken Aunt Margarine could be addressing such words to her; it frightened her so much that she did not dare to answer, and just then Cathie and Belle came into the room.

'Oh, mother,' they began penitently, 'we're so sorry, but we couldn't find dear Prissie anywhere, so we haven't picked up anything the whole afternoon!'

'Ah, my poor darlings, you shall never be your cousin's slaves any more. Don't go near her, she's a naughty, deceitful wretch; her jewels are false, my sweet loves, false! She has imposed upon us all, she does not deserve to associate with you!'

'I always said Prissie's jewels looked like the things you get on crackers!' said Belle, tossing her head.

'Now we shall have a little rest, I hope,' chimed in Cathie.

'I shall send her home to her parents this very night,' declared Aunt Margarine; 'she shall not stay here to pervert our happy household with her miserable gewgaws!'

Here Priscilla found her tongue. 'Do you think I want to stay?' she said proudly; 'I see now that you only wanted to have me here because—because of the horrid jewels, and I never knew they were false, and I let you have them all, every one, you know I did; and I wanted you to mind what I said and not trouble about picking them up, but you would do it! And now you all turn round upon me like this! What have I done to be treated so? What have I done?'

'Bravo, Prissie!' cried Dick. 'Mother, if you ask me, I think it serves us all jolly well right, and it's a downright shame to bullyrag poor Prissie in this way!'

'I don't ask you,' retorted his mother, sharply; 'so you will kindly keep your opinions to yourself.'

'Tra-la-la!' sang rude Dick, 'we are a united family—we are, we are, we are!'—a vulgar refrain he had picked up at one of the burlesque theatres he was only too fond of frequenting.

But Priscilla came to him and held out her hand quite gratefully and humbly. 'Thank you, Dick,' she said; 'you are kind, at all events. And I am sorry you couldn't have your horse-shoe pin!'

'Oh, hang the horse-shoe pin!' exclaimed Dick, and poor Priscilla was so thoroughly cast down that she quite forgot to reprove him.

She was not sent home that night after all, for Dick protested against it in such strong terms that even Aunt Margarine saw that she must give way; but early on the following morning Priscilla quitted her aunt's house, leaving her belongings to be sent on after her.

She had not far to walk, and it so happened that her way led through the identical lane in which she had met the fairy. Wonderful to relate, there, on the very same stone and in precisely the same attitude, sat the old lady, peering out from under her poke-bonnet, and resting her knotty old hands on her crutch-handled stick!

Priscilla walked past with her head in the air, pretending not to notice her, for she considered that the fairy had played her a most malicious and ill-natured trick.

'Heyday!' said the old lady (it is only fairies who can permit themselves such old-fashioned expressions nowadays). 'Heyday, why, here's my good little girl again! Isn't she going to speak to me?'

'No, she's not,' said Priscilla—but she found herself compelled to stop, notwithstanding.

'Why, what's all this about? You're not going to sulk with me, my dear, are you?'

'I think you're a very cruel, bad, unkind old woman for deceiving me like this!'

'Goodness me! Why, didn't the jewels come, after all?'

'Yes—they came, only they were all horrid artificial ones—and it is a shame, it is!' cried poor Priscilla from her bursting heart.

'Artificial, were they? that really is very odd! Can you account for that at all, now?'

'Of course I can't! You told me that they would drop out whenever I said anything to improve people—and I was always saying something improving! Aunt had a bandbox in her room quite full of them.'

'Ah, you've been very industrious, evidently; it's unfortunate your jewels should all have been artificial—most unfortunate. I don't know how to explain it, unless'—(and here the old lady looked up queerly from under her white eyelashes), 'unless your goodness was artificial too?'

'How do you mean?' asked Priscilla, feeling strangely uncomfortable. 'I'm sure I've never done anything the least bit naughty—how can my goodness possibly be artificial?'

'Ah, that I can't explain; but I know this—that people who are really good are generally the last persons to suspect it, and the moment they become aware of it and begin to think how good they are, and how bad everybody else is, why, somehow or other, their goodness crumbles away and leaves only a sort of outside shell behind it. And—I'm very old, and of course I may be mistaken—but I think (I only say I think, mind) that a little girl so young as you must have some faults hidden about her somewhere, and that perhaps on the whole she would be better employed in trying to find them out and cure them before she attempted to correct those of other people. And I'm sure it can't be good for any child to be always seeing herself in a little picture, just as she likes to fancy other people see her. Very many pretty books are written about good little girls, and it is quite true that children may exercise a great influence for good—more than they can ever tell, perhaps—but only just so long as they remain natural and unconscious, and not unwholesome little pragmatical prigesses; for then they make themselves and other people worse than they might have been. But of course, my dear, you never made such a mistake as that!'

Priscilla turned very red, and began to scrape one of her feet against the other; she was thinking, and her thoughts were not at all pleasant ones.

'Oh, fairy,' she said at last, 'I'm afraid that's just what I did do. I was always thinking how good I was and putting everybody—papa, mamma, Alick, Betty, Aunt Margarine, Cathie, Belle, and even poor cousin Dick—right! I have been a horrid little hateful prig, and that's why all the jewels were rubbish. But, oh, shall I have to go on talking sham diamonds and things all the rest of my life?'

'That,' said the fairy, 'depends entirely on yourself. You have the remedy in your own hands—or lips.'

'Ah, you mean I needn't talk at all? But I must—sometimes. I couldn't bear to be dumb as long as I lived—and it would look so odd, too!'

'I never said you were not to open your lips at all. But can't you try to talk simply and naturally—not like little girls or boys in any story-books whatever—not to "show off" or improve people; only as a girl would talk who remembers that, after all, her elders are quite as likely as she is to know what they ought or ought not to do and say?'

'I shall forget sometimes, I know I shall!' said Priscilla disconsolately.

'If you do, there will be something to remind you, you know. And by and by, perhaps, as you grow up you may, quite by accident, say something sincere and noble and true—and then a jewel will fall which will really be of value!'

'No!' cried Priscilla, 'no, please! Oh, fairy, let me off that! If I must drop them, let them be false ones to punish me—not real. I don't want to be rewarded any more for being good—if I ever am really good!'

'Come,' said the fairy, with a much pleasanter smile, 'you are not a hopeless case, at all events. It shall be as you wish, then, and perhaps it will be the wisest arrangement for all parties. Now run away home, and see how little use you can make of your fairy gift.'

Priscilla found her family still at breakfast.

'Why,' observed her father, raising his eyebrows as she entered the room, 'here's our little monitor—(or is it monitress, eh, Priscilla?)—back again. Children, we shall all have to mind our p's and q's—and, indeed, our entire alphabet, now!'

'I'm sure,' said her mother, kissing her fondly, 'Priscilla knows we're all delighted to have her home!'

'I'm not,' said Alick, with all a boy's engaging candour.

'Nor am I,' added Betty, 'it's been ever so much nicer at home while she's been away!'

Priscilla burst into tears as she hid her face upon her mother's protecting shoulder. 'It's true!' she sobbed, 'I don't deserve that you should be glad to see me—I've been hateful and horrid, I know—but, oh, if you'll only forgive me and love me and put up with me a little, I'll try not to preach and be a prig any more—I will truly!'

And at this her father called her to his side and embraced her with a fervour he had not shown for a very long time.

I should not like to go so far as to assert that no imitation diamond, ruby, pearl, or emerald ever proceeded from Priscilla's lips again. Habits are not cured in a day, and fairies—however old they may be—are still fairies; so it did occasionally happen that a mock jewel made an unwelcome appearance after one of Priscilla's more unguarded utterances. But she was always frightfully ashamed and abashed by such an accident, and buried the imitation stones immediately in a corner of the garden. And as time went on the jewels grew smaller and smaller, and frequently dissolved upon her tongue, leaving a faintly bitter taste, until at last they ceased altogether and Priscilla became as pleasant and unaffected a girl as she who may now be finishing this history.

Aunt Margarine never sent back the contents of that bandbox; she kept the biggest stones and had a brooch made of them, while, as she never mentioned that they were false, no one out of the family ever so much as suspected it.

But, for all that, she always declared that her niece Priscilla had bitterly disappointed her expectations—which was perhaps the truest thing that Aunt Margarine ever said.

A Matter Of Taste

It is a little singular that, upon an engagement becoming known and being discussed by the friends and acquaintances of the persons principally concerned, by far the most usual tone of comment should be a sorrowing wonder. That particular alliance is generally the very last that anybody ever expected. 'What made him choose her, of all people,' and 'What on earth she could see in him,' are declared insoluble problems. It is confidently predicted that the engagement will never come to anything, or that, if such a marriage ever does take place, it is most unlikely to prove a success.

Sometimes, in the case of female friends, this tone is even perceptible under their warmest felicitations, and through the smiling mask of compliment shine eyes moist with the most irritating quality of compassion. 'So glad! so delighted! But why, why didn't you consult me?'—this complicated expression might be rendered: 'I could have saved you from this—I was so pleased to hear of it!'

And yet, in the majority of cases, these unions are not found to turn out so very badly after all, and the misguided couple seem really to have gauged their own hearts and their possibilities of happiness together more accurately than the most clear-sighted of their acquaintances.

The announcement that Ella Hylton had accepted George Chapman provoked the customary sensation and surprise in their respective sets, and perhaps with rather more justification than usual.

Miss Hylton had undeniable beauty of a spiritual and rather exalte type, and was generally understood to be highly cultivated. She had spent a year at Somerville, though she had gone down without trying for a place in either 'Mods.' or 'Greats,' thereby preserving, if not increasing, her reputation for superiority. She had lived all her life among cultured people; she was devoted to music and regularly attended the Richter Concerts, though she could seldom be induced to play in public; she had a feeling for art, though she neither painted nor drew; a love of literature strong enough to deter her from all amateur efforts in that direction. In art, music and literature she was impatient of mediocrity; and, while she was as fond as most girls of the pleasures which upper middle-class society can offer, she reverenced intellect, and preferred the conversation of the plainest celebrity to the platitudes of the mere dancing-man, no matter how handsome of feature and perfect of step he might be.

George Chapman was certainly not a mere dancing-man, his waltzing being rather conscientious than dreamlike, and he was only tolerably good-looking. On the other hand, he was not celebrated in any way, and even his mother and sisters had never considered him brilliant. He had been educated at Rugby and Trinity, Cambridge, where he rowed a fairly good oar, on principle, and took a middle second in the Moral Science Tripos. Now he was in a solicitor's office, where he was receiving a good salary, and was valued as a steady, sensible young fellow, who could be thoroughly depended upon. He was fond of his profession, and had acquired a considerable knowledge of its details; apart from it he had no very decided tastes; he lived a quiet, regular life, and dined out and went to dances in moderation; his manner, though he was nearly twenty-six, was still rather boyishly blunt.

What there was in him that had found favour in Ella Hylton's fastidious eyes the narrator is not rash enough to attempt to particularise. But it may be suggested that the most unlikely people may possess their fairy rose and ring which render them irresistible to at least one heart, if they only have faith to believe in and luck to perceive their power.

So, early in the year, George had plucked up courage to propose to Miss Hylton, after meeting and secretly adoring her for some months past, and she, to the general astonishment, had accepted him.

He had a private income—not a large one—of his own, and had saved out of it. She was entitled under her grandmother's will to a sum which made her an heiress in a modest way, and thus there was no reason why the engagement should be a long one, and, though no date had been definitely fixed for the marriage, it was understood that it should take place at some time before the end of the summer.

Soon after the engagement, however, an invalid aunt with whom Ella had always been a great favourite was ordered to the south of France, and implored her to go with her; which Ella, who had a real affection for her relative, as well as a strong sense of duty, had consented to do.

This was a misfortune in one of two ways: it either curtailed that most necessary and most delightful period during which fiances discover one another's idiosyncrasies and weaknesses, or it made it necessary to postpone the marriage.

George naturally preferred the former, as the more endurable evil; but Ella's letters from abroad began to hint more and more plainly at delay. Her aunt might remain on the Continent all the summer, and she could not possibly leave her; there was so much to be done after her return that could not be done in a hurry; they had not even begun to furnish the pretty little house on Campden Hill that was to be their new home—it would be better to wait till November, or even later.

The mere idea was alarming to George, and he remonstrated as far as he dared; but Ella remained firm, and he grew desperate.

He might have spared himself the trouble. About the middle of June Ella's aunt—who, of course, had had to leave the Riviera—grew tired of travelling, and Ella, to George's intense satisfaction, returned to her mother's house in Linden Gardens, Notting Hill.

And now, when our story opens, George, who had managed to get away from office-work two hours before his usual time, was hurrying towards Linden Gardens as fast as a hansom could take him, to see his betrothed for the first time after their long separation.

He was eager, naturally, and a little nervous. Would Ella still persist in her wish for delay? or would he be able to convince her that there were no obstacles in the way? He felt he had strong arguments on his side, if only—and here was the real seat of his anxiety—if only her objections were not raised from some other motive! She might have been trying to prepare him for a final rupture, and then—'Well,' he concluded, with his customary good sense, 'no use meeting trouble halfway—in five minutes I shall know for certain!'

At the same moment Mrs. Hylton and her daughter Flossie, a vivacious girl in the transitory sixteen-year-old stage, were in the drawing-room at Linden Gardens. It was the ordinary double drawing-room of a London house, but everything in it was beautiful and harmonious. The eye was vaguely rested by the delicate and subdued colour of walls and hangings; cabinets, antique Persian pottery, rare bits of china, all occupied the precise place in which their decorative value was most felt; a room, in short, of exceptional individuality and distinction.

Flossie was standing at the window, from which a glimpse could just be caught of fresh green foliage and the lodge-gates, with the bustle of the traffic in the High Street beyond; Mrs. Hylton was writing at a Flemish bureau in the corner.

'I suppose,' said Flossie meditatively, as she fingered a piece of old stained glass that was hanging in the window, 'we shall have George here this afternoon.'

Mrs. Hylton raised her head. She had a striking face, tinted a clear olive, with a high wave of silver hair crowning the forehead; her eyebrows were dark, and so were the brilliant eyes; the nose was aquiline, and the thin, well-cut mouth a little hard. She was a woman who had been much admired in her time, and who still retained a certain attraction, though some were apt to find her somewhat cold and unsympathetic. Her daughter Ella, for example, was always secretly a little in awe of her mother, who, however, had no terrors for audacious, outspoken Flossie.

'If he comes, Flossie, he will be very welcome,' she said, 'but I hardly expect him yet. George is not likely to neglect his duties, even for Ella.'

Flossie pursed her mouth rather scornfully: 'Oh, George is immaculate!' she murmured.

'If he was, it would hardly be a reproach,' said her mother, catching the word; 'but, at all events, George has thoroughly good principles, and is sure to succeed in the world. I have every reason to be pleased.'

'Every reason?—ah! but are you pleased? Mother, dear, you know he's as dull as dull!'

'Ella does not find him so—and, Flossie, I don't like to hear you say such things, even in Ella's absence.'

'Oh, I never abuse him to Ella; it wouldn't be any use: she's firmly convinced that he's perfection—at least she was before she went away.'

'Why? do you mean that she has altered?—have you seen any sign of it, Flossie?'

Mrs. Hylton made this inquiry sharply, but not as if such a circumstance would be altogether displeasing to her.

'Oh, no; only she hasn't seen him for so long, you know. Perhaps, when she comes to look at him with fresh eyes, she'll notice things more. Ah, here is George, just getting out of a hansom—so he has played truant for once! There's one thing I do think Ella might do—persuade him to shave off some of those straggly whiskers. I wonder why he never seems to get a hat or anything else like other people's!'

Presently George was announced. He was slightly above middle height, broad-shouldered and fresh-coloured; the obnoxious whiskers did indeed cover more of his cheeks than modern fashion prescribes for men of his age, and had evidently never known a razor; he wore a turn-down collar and a necktie of a rather crude red; his clothes were neat and well brushed, but not remarkable for their cut.

'Well, my dear George,' said Mrs. Hylton, 'we have seen very little of you while Ella has been away.'

'I know,' he said awkwardly; 'I've had a lot of things to look after in one way and another.'

'What? after your work at the office was over!' cried Flossie incredulously.

'Yes—after that; it's taken up my time a good deal.'

'And so you couldn't spare any to call here—I see!' said Flossie. 'George,' she added, with a sudden diversion, 'I wonder you aren't afraid of catching cold! How can you go about in such absurdly thin boots as those?'

'These?' he said, inspecting them doubtfully—they were strong, sensible boots with notched and projecting soles of ponderous thickness—'why, what's the matter with them, Flossie, eh? Don't you think they're strong enough for walking in?'

'No, George; they're the very things for an afternoon dance, and quite a lot of couples could dance in them, you see. But for walking—ah, I'm afraid you sacrifice too much to appearances.'

'I don't, really!' George protested in all good faith; 'now do I, Mrs. Hylton?'

'Flossie is making fun of you, George; you mustn't mind her impertinence.'

'Oh, is that all? Do you know, I really thought for the moment that she meant they were too small for me! You like getting a rise out of me, Flossie, don't you?'

And he laughed with such genuine and good-natured amusement that the young lady felt somehow a little small, and almost ashamed, although it took the form of suppressed irritation. 'He really ought not to come here in such things,' she said to herself; 'and I don't believe that, even now, he sees what I meant.'

Just at this point Ella came in, with the least touch of shyness, perhaps, at meeting him before witnesses after so long an absence; but she only looked the more charming in consequence, and, demure as her greeting was, her pretty eyes had a sparkle of pleasure that scattered all George Chapman's fears to the winds. Even Flossie felt instinctively that straggly-whiskered, red-necktied, thick-booted George had lost none of his divinity for Ella.

They did not seem to have much to say to one another, notwithstanding; possibly because Ella was called upon to dispense the tea which had just been brought in. George sat nursing the hat which Flossie found so objectionable, while he balanced a teacup with the anxious eye of a juggler out of practice, and the conversation flagged. At last, under pretence of renewing his tea, most of which he had squandered upon a Persian rug, he crossed to Ella: 'I say,' he suggested, 'don't you think you could come out for a little while? I've such lots to tell you and—and I want you to go somewhere with me.'

Mrs. Hylton made no objection, beyond stipulating that Ella must not be allowed to tire herself after her journey, and so, a few minutes later, Miss Hylton came down in her pretty summer hat and light cape, and she and George were allowed to set out.

Once outside the house, he drew a long breath of mingled relief and pleasure: 'By Jove, Ella, I am glad to get you back again! I say, how jolly you do look in that hat! Now, do you know where I'm going to take you?'

'It will be quietest in the Gardens,' said Ella.

'Ah, but that's not where you're going now,' he said with a delicious assumption of authority; 'you're coming with me to see a certain house on Campden Hill you may have heard of.'

'That will be delightful. I do want to see our dear little house again very much. And, George, we will go carefully over all the rooms, and settle what can be done with each of them. Then we can begin directly; we haven't too much time.'

'Perhaps,' he said with a conscious laugh, 'it won't take so much time as you think.'

'Oh, but it must—to do properly. And while I've been away I've had some splendid ideas for some of the rooms—I've planned them out so beautifully. You know that delightful little room at the back?—the one I said should be your own den, with the window all festooned with creepers and looking out on the garden—well—?'

'Take my advice,' he said, 'and don't make any plans till you see it. And as for plans, these furnishing fellows do all that—they don't care to be bothered with plans.'

'They will have to carry out ours, though. I shall love settling how it is all to be—it will be such fun.'

'You wouldn't call it fun if you knew what it was like, I can tell you.'

'But I do know. Mother and I rearranged most of the rooms at home only last year—so you see I have some experience. And what experience can you have had, if you please?'

Ella had a mental vision as she spoke of the house in Dawson Place when George lived with his mother and sisters—a house in which furniture and everything else were commonplace and bourgeois to the last degree, and where nothing could have been altered since his boyhood; indeed she had often secretly pitied him for having to live in such surroundings, and admired the filial patience that had made him endure them so long.

'I've had my share, Ella, and I should be very sorry for you to have all the worry and bother I've been through over it!'

'But when, George? How? I don't understand.'

'Ah, that's my secret!' he said provokingly; 'and you know, Ella, if we began furnishing now, it would take no end of a time, with all these wonderful plans of yours, and—and I couldn't stand having to wait till next November for you—I couldn't do it!'

'Mother thinks the marriage need not be put off now,' said Ella simply, 'and we shall have six weeks till then; the house can be quite ready for us by the time we want it.'

'Six weeks!' he said impatiently, 'what's six weeks? You've no idea what these chaps are, Ella! And then there are all your own things to get, and they would take up most of your time. No, we should have had to put it off, whatever you may say. And that would mean another separation—for, of course, you would go away in August, and I should have to stay in town: the office wouldn't give me my fortnight twice over—honeymoon or no honeymoon!'

Ella looked completely puzzled. 'But what are you trying to prove now, George?'

'I was only showing you that, even though you have come back earlier, we couldn't possibly have got things ready in time, if I hadn't—' but here he stopped. 'No, I want that to be a surprise for you, Ella; you'll see presently,' he added.

Ella's delicate eyebrows contracted. 'I like to be prepared for my surprises, please, George. Tell me now.'

They had turned up one of the quiet streets leading to the hill. They were so near the house that George thought he might abandon further mystery, not to mention that he was only too anxious to reveal his secret.

'Well, then, Ella, if you must have it,' he said triumphantly, 'the house is very nearly ready now—what do you think of that?'

'Do you mean that—that it is furnished, George?'

'Papered, painted, decorated, furnished—everything, from top to bottom! I thought that would surprise you, Ella!'

'I think,' she answered slowly, 'you might have told me you were doing it.'

'What! before it was all done? That would have spoilt it all, dear. I should have written, though, if you hadn't been coming home so soon. And now it's finished I must say it looks uncommonly jolly. I'm sure you'll be pleased with it—it looks quite a different place.'

She tried to smile: 'And did you do it all yourself, George?'

'Well, no—not exactly. I flatter myself I know how to see that the work's properly done, and all that; but there are some things I don't pretend to be much of a hand at, so I got certain ladies to give me some wrinkles.'

Ella felt relieved. She was disappointed, it is true—hurt, even, at having been deprived of any voice in the matter. She had been looking forward so much to carrying out her pet schemes, to enjoying her friends' admiration of the wonders wrought by her artistic invention. And she had never thought of George, somehow, as likely to have any strikingly original ideas on the subject of decoration, although she liked him none the less for that.

But it was something that he had had the good sense to take her mother and Flossie into his confidence: she knew she could trust them to preserve him from any serious mistakes.

'You see,' said George, half apologetically, 'I would ever so much rather have waited till you came back, only I couldn't tell when that would be. I really couldn't help myself. You're sure you don't mind about it? If you only knew how I worked over it, rushing about from one place to another, as soon as I could get away from the office, picking up bits of furniture here and there, standing over those beggars of painters and keeping 'em at it, and working out estimates and seeing foremen and managers and all kinds of chaps! I used to get home dead-tired of an evening; but I didn't mind that: I felt it was all bringing you nearer to me, darling, and that made everything a pleasure!'

There was such honest affection in his look and voice; he had so evidently intended to please her, and had been in such manifest dread of any further separation from her, that she was completely disarmed.

'Dear George,' she said gently, 'I am so sorry you took all the trouble on yourself; it was very, very good of you to care so much, and I know I shall be delighted with the house.'

'Well,' said George, 'I'm not much afraid about that, because I expect our tastes are pretty much the same in most things.'

They were by this time at the house, and George, after a little fumbling with his as yet unfamiliar latchkey, threw open the door with a flourish and said, 'There you are, little woman! Walk in and you'll see what you shall see!'

No sooner was Ella inside the hall than her heart sank: 'Looks neat and nice, doesn't it?' said George cheerfully. 'You'd almost take that paper for real marble, wouldn't you? See how well they've done those veins. I like this yellowish colour better than green, don't you? It looks so cool in summer. That's a good strong hall-lamp—not what you call high art, exactly—but gives a rattling good light, and that's the main thing. Here, I'll light it up for you—confound it! they haven't turned the gas on yet. However, there's too much sunshine for it to show much, if they had. This linoleum is a capital thing: you might scrub as long as you liked and you'd never get that pattern out!'

'No,' Ella agreed, with a tragic little smile, 'it—it looks as if it would last.'

'Last! I should just think so! And here's a hatstand—you could almost swear it was carved wood of some sort, but it's only cast-iron painted; indestructible, you see; they told me that was the latest dodge—wonderful how cheaply they turn them out, isn't it?'

'I thought you said you were helped?'

'Oh, I didn't want any help here—this is only the passage, you know!'

Yes, it was only the passage—and yet she had been picturing such a charming entrance, with a draped arch, a graceful lamp, a fresh bright paper, a small buffet of genuine old oak, and so on. She suppressed a sigh as she passed on; after all, so long as the rooms themselves were all right, it did not so very much matter, and she knew that her mother's taste could be trusted.

But on the threshold of the dining-room she stopped aghast. The walls had been distempered a particularly hideous drab; the curtains were mustard yellow; the carpet was a dull brown; the mottled marble mantelpiece, for which she had been intending to substitute one in walnut wood with tiles, still shone in slabs of petrified brawn; there was a huge mahogany sideboard of a kind she had only seen in old-fashioned hotels.

'Comfortable, eh?' remarked George. 'Lots of wear in those curtains!'

Unhappily there was, as Ella was only too well aware. 'You did this room yourself too, then, George?' she managed to say, without betraying herself by her voice.

'Yes, I chose everything here. You see, Ella, we shall only use this room for meals.'

'Only for meals, yes,' she acquiesced with a shudder; 'but—George, surely you said mother had helped you with the rooms?'

'What! your mother? No, Ella; her notions are rather too grand for me. It was Jessie and Carrie I meant. Just come and see what they've made of my den.'

Ella followed. The window—which had commanded such a cheerful outlook into one of the pretty gardens, with a pink thorn, a laburnum-tree or two, and some sycamores which still flourish fresh and fair on Campden Hill—was obscured now by some detestable contrivance in transparent paper imitating stained glass.

'That was the girls' notion,' said George, following the direction of her eyes; 'they fixed it all themselves—it was their present to me. Pretty of them to think of it, wasn't it? I call it an immense improvement, and, you see, it's stuck on with some patent cement varnish, so it can't rub off. You get the effect better if you stand here—now, see how well the colours come out in the sun!'

If only they would come out! But what could she do but stand and admire hypocritically? Her eyes, in spite of herself, seemed drawn to that bright-hued sham intersected by black lines intended to represent leading; of the room itself she only saw vaguely that it was not unworthy of the window.

'Nothing to what they've done with the drawing-room!' said innocent George, beaming; 'come along, darling, you'll scarcely know the place.'

And Ella, reduced to a condition of stony stupor, followed to the drawing-room. She did not know the place, indeed. It was a quaintly-shaped, irregular room, with French windows opening upon the garden on one side and a deep bow-window on another; when she had last seen it, the walls were covered with a paper so pleasing in tone and design that she had almost decided to retain it. That paper was gone, and in its place a gaudy semi-Chinese pattern of unknown birds, flying and perching on sprawling branches laden with impossible flowers. And then the furniture—the 'elegant drawing-room suite' in brilliant plush and shiny satin, the cheap cabinets, and the ready-made black and gilt overmantel, with its panels of swans, hawthorn-blossom, and landscapes sketchily daubed on dead gold—surely it had all been transferred bodily from the stage of some carelessly mounted farcical comedy!

Ella's horrified gaze gradually took in other features—the china monkeys swinging on cords, the porcelain parrots hanging in great brass rings, huge misshapen terra-cotta jars and pots, dead grass in bloated drain-pipes, tambourines, beribboned and painted with kittens and robins, enormous wooden sabots, gilded Japanese fans, a woolly white rug and a bright Kidderminster carpet.

'Oh, George!' burst involuntarily from her lips.

'I knew you'd be pleased!' he said complacently; 'but I mustn't take all the credit myself. It was like this, you see: I felt all right enough about the other rooms, but the drawing-room—that's your room, and I was awfully afraid of not having it exactly as it ought to be. So I went to the girls, and I said, "You know all about these things—just make it what you think Ella will like, and then we can't go wrong!" We had that Grosvenor Gallery paper down first of all. "Choose something bright and cheerful," I said, and I don't think they've chosen badly. Then the pottery and china and all that—those are the girls' presents to you, with their best love.'

'It—it's very good of them,' said poor Ella, on the verge of tears.

'Oh, they think a lot of you! They were rather nervous about doing anything at first, for fear you mightn't like it; but I told them they needn't be afraid. "What I like, Ella will like," I said; and, I must say, no one could wish to see a prettier drawing-room than they've turned it into—they've a good deal of taste, those two girls.'

Ella stood there in a kind of dreary dream. What had happened to the world since she came into this house? What was this change in her? She was afraid to speak, lest the intense rebellious anger she felt should gain the mastery. Was it she that had these wicked thoughts of George—poor, kind, unsuspecting, loving George? She felt a little faint, for the windows were closed and the room stuffy with the odour of the new furniture and the atmosphere of the workshop; everything here seemed to her commonplace and repulsive.

'How about those plans of yours now, Ella, eh?' cried George.

This was too much; her overtried patience broke down. 'George!' she cried impulsively, and her voice sounded hoarse and strange to her own ear; 'George! I must speak—I must tell you!—' and then she checked herself. She must keep command of herself, or she could not, without utter loss of dignity, find the words that were to sting him into a sense of what he had done and allowed to be done. Before she could go on, George had drawn her to him, and was patting her shoulder tenderly. 'I know, dear little girl,' he said, 'I know; don't try to tell me anything. I'm so awfully glad you're pleased; but all the money and pains in the world wouldn't make the place good enough for my Ella!'

She released herself with a little cry of impotent despair. How could she say the sharp, cruel speeches that were struggling to reach her tongue now? It was no use; she was a coward; she simply had not the courage to undeceive him here, on the very first day of their reunion, too!

'You haven't been upstairs yet,' said George, dropping sentiment abruptly; 'shall we go up?'

Ella assented submissively, much as even this cost her; but it was better, she reflected, to get it over and know the very worst. However, she was spared this ordeal for the present; as they returned to the hall, they found themselves suddenly face to face with a dingy man, whose face was surrounded by a fringe of black whiskers and crowned by a shock of fleecy hair.

'Who on earth are you?' demanded George, as the man rose from the kitchen-stairs.

'No offence, sir and lady! Peagrum, that's my name, fust shop round the corner as you go into Silver Street, plumber and sanitry hengineer, gas-fittin' and hartistic decorating, bell-'anging in all its branches. I received instructions from Mr. Jones that I was to look into a little matter o' leakage in the back-kitchen sink; also to see what taps, if hany, required seein' to, and gen'ally to put things straight like. So I come round, 'aving the keys, jest to cast a heye over them, as I may term it, preliminry to commencing work in the course of a week or so, as soon as I'm at libity to attend to it pussonally.'

'Oh, the landlord sent you? All right, then.'

'Correct, sir,' said the plumber affably. 'While I've been 'ere, I took the freedom of going all over this little 'ouse, and a nice cosy little 'ouse you've made of it, for such a nouse as it is! You've done it up very tysty—very tysty you've done this little 'ouse up; and I've some claim to speak, seein' as how I've had the decoration throughout of a many 'ouses in my time, likewise mansions. You ain't been too ambitious, which is the error most parties falls into with small 'ouses. Now the parties as 'ad the place before you—by the name o' Rummles—well, I daresay they satisfied theirselves, but the 'ouse never looked right—not to my taste, it didn't!'

'George, get rid of this person!' said Ella rapidly, under her breath, in French. Unfortunately, George's acquaintance with that tongue was about on a par with the plumber's, and he remained passive.

The plumber now proceeded to put down his mechanic's straw-bag upon the hall-table, which he did with great care, as if it were of priceless stuff and contained fragile articles; having done this, he posed himself with one elbow resting on the post at the foot of the staircase, like a grimy statue of Shakespeare.

'Ah,' he said, shaking his touzled head, 'this ain't the fust time I've been 'ere in my puffessional capacity, not by a long way. Not by a long way, it ain't. Mr. Rummles, him as I mentioned to you afore, and a nice pleasant-spoken gentleman he was, too—in the tea trade—Mr. Rummles, he allus sent round for me whenever there was hany odd jobs as wanted doin', and in course I was allus pleased to get 'em, be they hodd or hotherwise.'

'Er-exactly,' said George, as soon as he could put in a word; 'but you see, this lady and I—'

The plumber, however, did not abandon his position, and seemed determined that they should hear him:

'I know, sir—I see how things were with you with 'arf a glance; but afore we go any further, it's right you should know 'oo I am and all about me. Jest 'ear what I'm goin' to tell you, for it's somethink out of the common way, though gospel-truth. It's a melinkly reflection for a man in my station of life, but'—and here he lowered his voice to a solemn pitch—'I've never set foot inside of this 'ere 'ouse without somethink 'appens more or less immejit. Ah, it's true, though. Seems almost like as if I brought a fatality in along o' me. Don't you interrupt; you wait till I'm done, and see if I'm talking at random or without facks to support me. Well, fust time as ever I was sent for 'ere was in regard to drains, as they couldn't flush satisfactory. I did my work and come away. Not three weeks arter, Miss Rummles, the heldest gell, was took ill with typhoid. Never the same young lady again—nor yet she never won't be neither, not if she lives to a nundered. "Nothing very hodd about that?" says you. Wait a bit. Next time, it was the kitching copper as had got all furred up like. I tinkered that up to rights, and come away. Well, afore I'd even made out my account, that identical copper blew up and scalded the cook dreadful! "Coppers will play these games," you sez. All right, then; but you let me finish. Third time there was a flaw in one of the gas-brackets in the spare room. I soddered it up and I come away. Soon arterwards, a day or two as it might be, Mrs. Rummles 'ad 'er mar a-stayin' with her, and the old lady slep in that very room, and was laid up weeks! "Curus," says I, when I come to 'ear of it, "very curus!" and it set me a-thinkin'. Last time but one—'ere, lemme see—that was a bell-'anging job, I think—no, I'm wrong, it was drains agen, so it were—drains it was agen. And the next thing I 'eard was that Mrs. Rummles was a-layin' at death's door with the diffthery! The last time—ah, I recklect well, I was called in to see if somethink wasn't wrong with the ballcock in the top cistin. I see there was somethink, and I come away as usual. That day week, old Mr. Rummles was took with a fit on the floor in the back droring-room, which broke up the 'ouse!

'Now, I think, as fair-minded and unprejudiced parties, you'll agree with me that there was something more'n hordinary coinside-ency in all that. I declare to you!' avowed the plumber, with a gloomy relish and a candour that was possibly begotten of beer, 'I declare to you there's times when I do honestly believe as I carry a curse along with me whenever I visits this 'ere partickler 'ouse! and, though it's agen my own hinterests, I deem it on'y my dooty, as a honest man, to mention it!'

Under any other circumstances, the plumber's compliments on her taste and his lugubrious assumption of character of the Destroying Angel would have sorely tried, if not completely upset, Ella's gravity; as it was, she was too wretched to have more than a passing and quite unappreciative sense of his absurdity. George, having the quality of mind which makes jokes more readily than sees them, took him quite seriously.

'Well,' he answered solemnly, 'I hope you won't bring us bad luck, at all events!'

'I 'ope so, sir, I'm sure. I 'ope so. It will not be by any desire on my part, more partickler when you're just settin' up 'ousekeepin' with your good lady 'ere. But there's no tellin' in these matters. That's where it is, you see—there's no tellin'. And, arter all my experence, with the best intentions in the world, I can't go and guarantee to you as nothink won't come of it. I wish I could, but, as a honest man, I can't. If it's to be,' moralised this fatalistic plumber, 'it is to be, and that's all about it, and no hefforts on my part or yours won't make hany difference, will they, sir?'

'Well, well,' said George, plainly ill at ease, 'that will do, my friend. Now, Ella, what do you say—shall we go upstairs?'

'Not now,' she gasped, 'let us go away—. Oh, George, take me outside, please!'

'Dash that confounded fool of a plumber!' said George, irritably, when they were in the street again; 'wonder if he thinks I'm going to employ him after that! Not that it isn't all bosh, of course—Why, Ella, you're not tired, are you?'

'I—I think I am a little—do you mind if we drive home?'

Ella was very silent during their short drive. When they reached Linden Gardens she said, 'I think we must say good-bye here, George. I feel as if I were going to have a headache.'

'You poor little girl!' he said, looking rather crestfallen, for he had been counting upon going in and being invited to remain for dinner, 'it's been rather too much for you, going over the house and all that—or was it that beastly plumber with his rigmaroles?'

'It wasn't the plumber,' she said hurriedly, as the door was opened, 'and—good-bye, George.'

'How easily girls do get knocked up!' thought George, as he walked homeward, 'a little pleasant excitement like this and she seems quite upset. She was delighted with the house, though, that's one blessing, and I mustn't forget to tell the girls how touched she was by their presents. What a darling she is, and how happy we shall be together!'

PART II

Once safely at home, Ella hastened upstairs to her own room, where, if the truth must be told, she employed the half-hour before dinner in unintermittent sobbing, into which temper largely entered. 'He has spoilt it all for me! How could he—oh, how could he?' ran the burden of her moan. At the dinner-table, though pale and silent, she had recovered composure.

'A pleasant walk, Ella?' inquired her mother, with rather formal interest.

'Yes, very,' replied Ella, trusting she would not be questioned further.

'I believe I know where you went!' cried indiscreet Flossie. 'You went to look at your new home—now, didn't you? Ah, I thought so! I suppose you have quite made up your minds how you mean to do the rooms?'

'Quite.'

'We might go round to all the best places to-morrow,' said Mrs. Hylton, 'and see some papers and hangings—there were some lovely patterns in Blank's windows the other day.'

'And, Ella,' added Flossie, 'I've been out with Andrews after school several times, to Tottenham Court Road, and Wardour Street, and Oxford Street—oh, everywhere, hunting up old furniture, and I can show you where they have some beautiful things—not shams, but really good!'

'You know, Ella,' said Mrs. Hylton, observing that she did not answer, 'I want you to have a pretty house, and you and George must order exactly what you like; but I think you will find I may be some help to you in choosing.'

'Thank you, mother,' said Ella, without any animation; 'I—I don't think we shall want much.'

'You will want all that young people in your position do want, I suppose,' said Mrs. Hylton, a little impatiently; 'and of course you understand that the bills are to be my affair.'

'Thank you, mother,' murmured Ella again. She didn't feel able to tell them just yet how this had all been forestalled; she felt that she would infallibly break down if she tried.

'You seem a little overdone to-night, my dear,' said her mother frigidly; she was naturally hurt at the very uneffusive way in which her good offices had been met.

'I have such a dreadful headache,' pleaded Ella. 'I—I think I overtired myself this afternoon.'

'Then you were very foolish, after travelling all yesterday, as you did. I don't wonder that George was ashamed to come in. You had better go to bed early, and I will send Andrews in to you with some of my sleeping mixture.'

Ella was glad enough to obey, though the draught took some time to operate; she felt as if no happiness or peace of mind were possible for her till George had been persuaded to undo his work.

Surely he could not refuse when he knew that her mother was prepared to do everything for them at her own expense!

And here it began to dawn upon her what this would entail! George's words came back to her as if she heard them actually spoken. Did he not say that the house had been furnished out of his savings?

What was she asking him to do? To dismantle it entirely; to humiliate himself by going round to all the people he had dealt with, asking them as a favour to take back their goods, or else he must sell them as best he could for a fraction of their cost. Who was to refund him all he had so uselessly spent? Could she ask her mother to do so? Would he even consent to such an arrangement if it was proposed?

Then his sisters—how could she avoid offending them irreparably, perhaps involving George in a quarrel with his family, if she were to carry her point?

As she realised, for the first time, the inevitable consequences of success, she asked herself in despair what she ought to do—where her plain duty lay?

Did she love George—or was it all delusion, and was he less to her than mere superfluities, the fringe of life?

She did love him, in spite of any passing disloyalty of thought. She felt his sterling worth and goodness, even his weaknesses had something lovable in them for her.

And he had been planning, spending, working all this time to give her pleasure, and this was his reward! She had been within an ace of letting him see the cruel ingratitude that was in her heart! 'What a selfish wretch I have been!' she thought; 'but I won't be—no, I won't! George shall not be snubbed, hurt, estranged from his family on my account!'

No, she would suffer—she alone—and in silence. Never by a word would she betray to him the pain his well-intentioned action cost her. Not even to her mother and Flossie would she permit herself to utter the least complaint, lest they should insist upon opening George's eyes!

So, having arrived at this heroic resolve, in which she found a touch of the sublime that almost consoled her, the tears dried on her cheeks and Ella fell asleep at last.

Some readers, no doubt—though possibly few of our heroine's sex—will smile scornfully at this crumpled rose-leaf agony, this tempest in a Dresden teacup; and the writer is not concerned to deny that the situation has its ludicrous side.

But, for a girl brought up as Ella Hylton had been, in an artistic milieu, her eye insensibly trained to love all that was beautiful in colour and form, to be almost morbidly sensitive to ugliness and vulgarity—it was a very real and bitter struggle, a hard-won victory to come to such a decision as she formed. Life, Heaven knows, contains worse trials and deeper tragedies than this; but at least Ella's happy life had as yet known no harder.

And, so far, she must be given the credit of having conquered.

Resolution is, no doubt, half the battle. Unfortunately, Ella's resolution, though she hardly perceived this at present, could not be effected by one isolated and final act, but by a long chain of daily and hourly forbearances, the first break in which would undo all that had gone before.

How she bore the test we are going to see.

She woke the next morning to a sense that her life had somehow lost its savour; the exaltation of her resolve overnight had gone off and left her spirits flat and dead; but she came down, nevertheless, determined to be staunch and true to George under all provocations.

'Have you and George decided when you would like your wedding to be?' asked her mother, after breakfast, 'because we ought to have the invitations printed very soon.'

'Not yet,' faltered Ella, and the words might have passed either as an answer or an appeal.

'I think it should be some time before the end of next month, or people will be going out of town.'

'I suppose so,' was the reply, so listlessly given that Mrs. Hylton glanced keenly at her daughter.

'What do you feel about it yourself, Ella?'

'I? oh, I—I've no feeling. Perhaps, if we waited—no, it doesn't matter—let it be when you and George wish, mother, please!'

Mrs. Hylton gave a sharp, annoyed little laugh: 'Really, my dear, if you can't get up any more interest in it than that, I think it would certainly be wiser to wait!'

It was more than indifference that Ella felt—a wild aversion to beginning the new life that but lately had seemed so mysteriously sweet and strange; she was frightened by it, ashamed of it, but she could not help herself. She made no answer, nor did Mrs. Hylton again refer to the subject.

But Ella's worst tribulations had yet to come. That afternoon, as she and her mother and Flossie were sitting in the drawing-room, 'Mrs. and the Miss Chapmans' were announced. Evidently they had deemed it incumbent on them to pay a state visit as soon as possible after Ella's return.

Ella returned their effusive greetings as dutifully as she could. She had never succeeded in cultivating a very lively affection for them; to-day she found them barely endurable.

Mrs. Chapman was a stout, dewlapped old lady, with dull eyes and pachydermatous folds in her face. She had a husky voice and a funereal manner. Jessie, her eldest daughter, was not altogether uncomely in a commonplace way: she was dark-haired, high-coloured, loud-voiced—generally sprightly and voluble and overpowering; she was in such a hurry to speak that her words tripped one another up, and she had a meaningless and, to Ella, highly irritating little laugh.

Carrie was plain and colourless, content to admire and echo her sister.

After some conversation on Ella's Continental experiences, Jessie suddenly, as Ella's uneasy instinct foresaw, turned to Mrs. Hylton. 'Of course, Ella told you what a surprise she had at Campden Hill yesterday? Weren't you electrified?'

'No doubt I should have been,' said Mrs. Hylton, who detested Jessie, 'only Ella did not think fit to mention it.'

'Oh, I wonder at that! I hope I wasn't going to betray the secrets of the prison-house?' Jessie was fond of using stock phrases to give lightness and sparkle to her conversation. 'Ella, the idea of your keeping it all to yourself, you sly puss! But tell me—would you ever have believed Tumps'—his sisters called George 'Tumps'—'could be capable of such independent behaviour?'

'No,' said Ella, 'I—indeed I never should!'

'Ha, ha! nor should we! You would have screamed to see him fussing about—wasn't he killing over it, Carrie?'

'Oh, he was, Jessie!'

'My son,' explained Mrs. Chapman to Mrs. Hylton, 'is so wonderfully energetic and practical. I have never known him fail to carry through anything he has once undertaken—he inherits that from his poor dear father.'

'I don't quite gather what your brother George has been doing, even now?' said Mrs. Hylton to Jessie.

'Oh, but my lips are sealed. Wild horses sha'n't drag any more from me! Don't be afraid, Ella, I won't spoil sport!'

'There is no sport to spoil,' said Ella. 'Mother, it is only that—that George has furnished the house while I have been away.'

'Really?' said Mrs. Hylton politely; 'that is energetic of him, indeed!'

'Poor dear Tumps came home so proud of your approval,' said Jessie to Ella, 'and we were awfully relieved to find you didn't think we'd made the house quite too dreadful—weren't we, Carrie?'

'Yes, indeed, Jessie.'

'Of course,' observed the latter young lady, 'it's always so hard to hit upon another person's taste exactly—especially in furnishing.'

'Impossible, I should have thought,' from Mrs. Hylton.

'I hope Ella is of a different opinion—what do you say, dearest?'

'Oh,' cried Ella hastily, with splendid mendacity, 'I—I liked it all very much, and—and it was so much too kind of you and Carrie. I've never thanked you for—for all the things you gave me!'

'Oh, those! they ain't worth thanking for—just a few little artistic odds and ends. They set off a room, you know—give it a finish.'

'Young people nowadays,' croaked old Mrs. Chapman lugubriously in Mrs. Hylton's courteously inclined ear, 'think so much of luxury and ornament. I'm sure when I married my dear husband, we—'

'Now, mater dear, you really mustn't!' interrupted the irrepressible Jessie; 'Mrs. Hylton is on our side, you know. She likes pretty things about her—don't you, Mrs. Hylton? And, talking of that, Ella, I hope you thought our glyco-vitrine decoration a success? We were perfectly surprised ourselves to see how well it came out! Just transparent coloured paper, Mrs. Hylton, and you cut it into sheets, and gum it on the window-panes, and really, unless you were told or came quite close, you would declare it was real stained glass! You ought to try some of it on your windows, Mrs. Hylton. I'll tell you where you can get it—you go down—'

'I'm afraid I'm old-fashioned, my dear,' said Mrs. Hylton, stiffly; 'if I cannot have the reality, I prefer to do without even the best imitations.'

'Why, you're deserting us, I declare! Ella, you must take her to see the window, and then perhaps she will change her opinion.'

'I always tell my girls,' said Mrs. Chapman, in her woolly voice, 'when I am dead and gone they can make any alterations they please, but while I am spared to them I like everything about the house to be kept exactly as it was in their poor father's lifetime.'

'Isn't she a dear conservative old mummy?' said Jessie to Ella in an audible aside. 'Why, I do believe she won't see anything to admire in your little house—at least, if she does, the dear old lady, she'd sooner die than admit it!'

The Chapmans went at last, and before they were out of the house Mrs. Hylton, with an effort to seem unconcerned, said: 'And so, Ella, you and George have done without my help? Of course you know your own affairs best; still, I should have thought—I should certainly have thought—that I might have been of some assistance to you—if only in pecuniary matters.'

'George preferred that you should not be troubled,' stammered Ella.

'I am not blaming him. I respect him for wishing to be independent. I own to being a little surprised that you should not have told me of this before, though, Ella. But for that chattering girl, I presume I should have been left to discover it for myself. I wonder you cannot bring yourself to be a little more open with your mother, my dear.'

'Oh, mother!' cried Ella in despair, 'indeed I was going to tell you—only, I did not know myself till yesterday. At least, that is—' she broke off lamely, fearing to reflect on George.

'I find it hard to believe that George would act without consulting you in any way. It is strange enough that he should have undertaken to furnish the house in your absence.'

'But if I couldn't be there!' pleaded Ella—'and I couldn't.'

'Naturally, as you were on the Continent, you couldn't be on Campden Hill at the same time; you need not be absurd, Ella. But what I want to know is this—have you had a voice in the matter, or have you not?'

'N—not much,' confessed Ella, hanging her head.

'So I suspected, and I think George ought to be ashamed of himself. I never heard of such a thing, and I shall make a point of seeing the house and satisfying myself that it is fit for a daughter of mine to inhabit.'

'Mother!' exclaimed Ella, springing up excitedly, 'you don't understand. Why should you choose to suppose that the house is not pretty? It is not done as you would do it, because poor George hadn't much money to spend; but if I am satisfied, why should you come between us? And I am satisfied—quite, quite satisfied; he has done it all beautifully, and I will not have a single thing altered! After all, it is his house—our house—and nobody else has any right to interfere—not even you, mother!'

Mrs. Hylton shrugged her shoulders. 'Oh, my dear, if that is the way you think proper to speak to me, it is time to change the subject. Pray understand that I shall not dream of interfering. I am very glad that you are so satisfied.' And by-and-by she left the room majestically.

When she had gone, Flossie, who had been listening open-eyed to all that had taken place, came and stood in front of Ella's chair.

'Ella, tell me,' she said, 'has George really furnished the house exactly as you like—really now?'

'Haven't I said so, Flossie? Why should you doubt it?'

'Oh, I don't know; I was wondering, that was all!'

'Really!' cried Ella angrily, 'anyone would think poor George was a sort of barbarian, who couldn't be expected to know anything, or trusted to do anything!'

'I'm sure I never said so, Ella. But how clever of him to choose just the right things! And, Ella, do all the colours and things go well together? I always thought most men didn't notice much about all that. And are the new mantelpieces pretty? Oh, and where did he go for the papers and the carpets?'

'Flossie, I wish you wouldn't tease so. Can't you see I have a headache? I can't answer so many questions, and I won't! Once for all, everything is just what I like. Do you understand, or shall I tell you again?—just, just what I like!'

'Oh, all right,' returned Flossie, with exasperating good-humour; 'then there's nothing to lose your temper about, darling, is there?'

And this was all that Ella had gained by her loyalty to George so far.

It was the morning after the Chapmans' visit. Ella had seen her mother and Flossie preparing to go out, but, owing to the friction between them, they neither invited her to accompany them, nor did she venture to ask where they were going. At luncheon, however, the unhappy girl divined from the expression of their faces how they had employed the forenoon. They had been inspecting the Campden Hill house! Her mother's handsome face wore a look of frozen contempt. Imagine a strict Quaker's feelings on seeing his son with a pair of black eyes—a Socialist's at finding a peerage under his daughter's pillow—a Positivist's whose children have all joined the Salvation Army, and even then but a faint idea will be reached of Mrs. Hylton's utter dismay and disgust.

Flossie, though angry, took a different view of Ella's share in the business; she knew her better than her mother did, and consequently refused to believe that she was a Philistine at heart. It was her absurd infatuation for George that made her see with his eyes and bow down before the hideous household gods he had chosen to erect. On such weakness Flossie had no mercy.

'Well, Ella, dear,' she began, 'mother and I have seen your house. George has quite surpassed our wildest expectations. Accept my compliments!'

'Flossie,' said her mother severely, 'will you kindly choose some other topic? I really feel too seriously annoyed about all this to bear to hear it spoken of just yet. I think you shall come with me to the Amberleys' garden-party this afternoon, and not Ella, as we are dining out this evening. You had better stay at home and rest, Ella.'

In this, and countless other ways, was Ella made to feel that she was in disgrace.

Nor did Flossie spare her sister when they were alone. 'Poor dear mother!' she said, 'I quite thought that house would have broken her heart—oh, I'm not saying a word against it, Ella, I know you like it, and I'm sure it looks very comfortable—everything so sensible and useful, and the kitchen really charming; mother and I liked it best of all the rooms. Such a horrid man let us in; he was at work there, and he would follow us all about, and tell mother his entire history. I don't think he could have been quite sober, he would insist on turning all the taps on everywhere. I suppose, Ella, it's ever so much cheaper to furnish as you and George have done; that's the worst of pretty things, they do cost such a lot! I'd no idea you were so practical, though,' and so on.

On Sunday George came to luncheon. He was delighted to hear from Flossie that they had been to the house, and gave a boisterously high-spirited account of his labours. 'It was a grind,' he informed them, 'and, as for those painter-fellows, I began to think they'd stay out the entire lease.'

'Art is long, George,' observed Flossie, wickedly.

'Oh yes, I know; but they promised faithfully to be out in ten days, and they were over three weeks!'

'But look at the result! George, how did you find out that Ella liked grained doors?'

'Well, to tell you the truth, Flossie, that was a bit of a fluke. The man told me that graining was coming in again, and I said, "Grain 'em, then"—I didn't know!'

In short, he was more provokingly dense than ever to-day, and Ella found herself growing more and more captious and irritable that afternoon; he could not understand why she was so disinclined to talk; even the dear little house of which she was so soon to be the mistress failed to interest her.

'You have told me twice already that you got the drawing-room carpet a great bargain, and only paid four pounds ten for the table in the dining-room,' she broke out. 'Can't we take that for granted in future?'

'I forgot I'd told you; I thought it was the mater,' he said; 'and I say, Ella, how about pictures? Jessie's promised to do us some water-colours—she's been taking lessons lately, you know—but we shall want one or two prints for the dining-room, shan't we? You can pick them up second-hand very cheap.'

'Oh yes, yes; anything you please, George!... No, no; I'm not cross, I'm only tired, especially of talking about the house. It is quite finished, you know, so what is there to discuss?'

During the days that followed, Flossie devised an ingenious method of tormenting Ella; she laid out her pocket-money, of which she had a good deal, on the most preposterous ornaments—a pair of dangling cut-glass lustres, bead mats, a trophy of wax fruit under a glass shade, gaudy fire-screens and flowerpots, all of which she solemnly presented to her suffering sister. This was not pure mischief or unkindness on Flossie's side, but part of a treatment she had hit upon for curing Ella of her folly. And at last the worm turned. Flossie came in one day with a cheap plush and terra-cotta panel of appalling ugliness.

'For the drawing-room, dear,' she observed blandly, and Ella suddenly burst into a flood of tears.

'You are very, very unkind to me, Flossie!' she sobbed.

'I!' exclaimed Flossie, in a tone of the most innocent surprise. 'Why, Ella, I thought you would be charmed with it. I'm sure George will. And, you know, it will go beautifully with the rest of your things!'

'You might understand ... you might see—'

'I might see what?'

'How frightfully miserable I am!' said Ella, which was the very admission Miss Flossie had been seeking to provoke.

'Suppose I do see,' she said; 'suppose I've been trying to get you to act sensibly, Ella?'

'Then it's cruel of you!'

'No it's not. It's kind. How am I to help you unless you speak out? I'm younger than you, Ella, but I know this—I would never mope and make myself miserable when a word would put everything right!'

'But it wouldn't, Flossie; it is too late to speak now. I can't tell him how I really feel—I can't!'

'Ah, then you own there is something to tell?'

'What have I said? Flossie, forget what I said; it slipped out. I meant nothing.'

'And you are perfectly happy and satisfied, are you? Now, I know how people look when they are perfectly happy and satisfied.'

'It's no use!' cried Ella, suddenly. 'I've tried, and tried, and tried to bear it, but I can't. I must tell somebody ... it is making me ill. I am getting cross and wicked, and unlike what I used to be. Flossie, I can't go and live there—I dread the thought of it; I shrink from it more and more every day! It is all odious, impossible—and yet I must, I must!'

'No, you mustn't; and, what's more, you shan't!'

'Flossie, you mean you will tell mother! You must not, do you hear? If you do, it will only make matters worse. Oh, why did I tell you?' cried Ella, in shame at this lapse from all her heroism. 'Promise me you will say nothing to mother—it is too late now—promise!'

'Very well,' said Flossie reluctantly; 'then I promise. But, all the same, Ella, I think you're a great goose!'

'I didn't promise I wouldn't say anything to George, though,' she reflected; and so, on the very next occasion that she caught him alone, she availed herself of an innocent allusion of his to Ella's low spirits to give him the benefit of her candid opinion, which was not tempered by any marked consideration for his feelings.

Ella was in the morning-room alone—she had taken to sitting alone lately, brooding over her trials. She was no heroine, after all; her mind, it is to be feared, was far from superior. She was finding out that she had undertaken too heavy a task; she could not console herself for her lost dream of a charmingly appointed house. She might endure to live in such a home as George had made for her; but to be expected to admire it, to let it be understood that it was her handiwork, that she had chosen or approved of it—this was the burden that was crushing her.

Suddenly the door opened and George stood before her. His expression was so altered that she scarcely recognised him; all the cheery buoyancy had vanished, and his stern, set face had a dignity and character in it now that were wanting before.

'I have just had a talk with Flossie,' he began; 'she has shown me what a—what a mistake I've been making.'

Ella could not help feeling a certain relief, though she said, 'It was very wrong of Flossie—she had no right to speak.'

'She had every right,' he said. 'She might have done it more kindly, perhaps, but that's nothing. Why didn't you tell me yourself, Ella? You might have trusted me!'

'I couldn't—it seemed so cruel, so ungrateful, after all you had done. I hoped you would never know.'

'It's well for you, and for me too, that I know this while there's still time. Ella, I've been a blind, blundering fool. I never had a suspicion of this till—till just now, or you don't think I should have gone on with it a single minute. I came to tell you that you need not make yourself miserable any longer. I will put an end to this—whatever it costs me.'

'Oh, George, I am so ashamed. I know it is weak and cowardly of me, but I can't help it. And—and will it cost you so very much?'

'Quite as much as I can bear.'

'No; but tell me—about how much? More than a hundred pounds?'

'I haven't worked it out in pounds, shillings, and pence,' he said grimly; 'but I should put it higher myself.'

'Won't they take back some of the things? They ought to,' she suggested timidly.

'The things? Oh, the furniture! Good Heavens, Ella! do you suppose I care a straw about that? All I can think of is how I could have gone on deceiving myself like this, believing I knew your every thought; and all the time—pah, what a fool I've been!'

'I thought I should get used to it,' she pleaded. 'And oh, you don't know how hard I have tried to bear it, not to let anyone see what I felt—you don't know!'

'And I would rather not know,' he replied, 'for it's not exactly flattering, you see, Ella. And at all events, it's over now. This is the last time I shall trouble you; you will see no more of me after to-day.'

Ella could only stare at him incredulously. Had he really taken the matter so seriously to heart as this? Could he not forgive the wound to his vanity? How hard, how utterly unworthy of him!

'Yes,' he continued, 'I see now we were quite unsuited to one another. I should never have made you happy, Ella; it's best to find it out before it's too late. So let us shake hands and say good-bye, my dear.'

She felt powerless to appeal to him, and yet it was not wholly pride that tied her tongue; she was too shaken and stunned to make the least effort at remonstrance.

'Then, if it must be,' she said at last, very low—'good-bye, George.'

He crushed her hand in his strong grasp. 'Don't mind about me,' he said roughly. 'You've nothing to blame yourself for. I daresay I shall get over it all right. It's rather sudden at first—that's all!' And with that he was gone.

Flossie, coming in a little later, found her sister sitting by the window, smiling in a strange, vacant way. 'Well?' said Flossie eagerly, for she had been anxiously waiting to hear the result of the interview.

'It's all over, Flossie; he has broken it off.'

'Oh, Ella, I'm so glad! I hoped he would, but I wasn't sure. Well, you may thank me for delivering you, darling. If I hadn't spoken plainly—'

'Tell me what you said.'

'Oh, let me see. Well, I told him anybody else would have seen long ago that your feelings were altered. I said you were perfectly miserable at having to marry him, only you thought it was too late to say so. I told him he didn't understand you in the least, and you hadn't a single thought or taste in common. I said if he cared about you at all, the best way he could prove it was by setting you free, and not spoiling your life and his own too. I put it as pleasantly as I could,' said Flossie naively, 'but he is very trying!'

'You told him all that! What made you invent such wicked, cruel lies? Flossie, it is you that have spoilt our lives, and I will never forgive you—never, as long as I live!'

'Ella!' cried the younger sister, utterly astonished at this outburst. 'Why, didn't you tell me the other day how miserable you were, and how you dared not speak about it? And now, when I—'

'Go away, Flossie; you have done mischief enough!'

'Oh, very well, I'm going—if this is all I get for helping you. Is it my fault if you don't know your own mind, and say what you don't mean? And if you really want your dearly beloved George back again, there's time yet; he hasn't gone—he's in the drawing-room with mother.'

How infinitely petty her past misery seemed now! for what trifles she had thrown away George's honest heart! If only there was a chance still! at least false pride should not come between them any longer: so thought Ella on her way to the drawing-room. George was still there; as she turned the door-handle she heard her mother's clear resonant tones. 'Not that that is any excuse for Ella,' she was saying.

Ella burst precipitately into the room. She was only just in time, for George had risen and was evidently on the point of leaving. 'George,' she exclaimed, panting after her rapid flight, 'I—I came to tell you—'

'My dear Ella,' interrupted Mrs. Hylton, 'the kindest thing you can do for George now is to let him go without any more explanations.'

Ella stopped; again her mind became a blank. What had she come for; what was it she felt she must say? While she hesitated, George was already at the other door; he seemed anxious to avoid hearing her; in another second he would be gone.

She cried to him piteously. 'George, dear George, don't leave me!... I can't bear it!'

'This is too ridiculous!' exclaimed her mother angrily. 'What is it that you do want, Ella?'

'I want George,' she said simply. 'It was all a mistake, George. Flossie mistook—Oh, you don't really think that I have left off caring for you? I haven't, dear, indeed I haven't—won't you believe me?'

'I had better leave you to come to an understanding together,' said Mrs. Hylton, not in the best of tempers, for she had been more sorry for George than for the rupture he came to announce, and she swept out of the room with very perceptible annoyance.

'I thought it was all up with me, Ella; I did indeed,' said George, a minute or two later, his face still pale after all this emotion. 'But tell me—what's wrong with the furniture I ordered?'

'Nothing, dear, nothing,' she answered, blushing. 'Don't think about it any more.'

'No? But your mother was talking about it too,' he insisted. 'Come, Ella, dear, for heaven's sake let us have no more misunderstandings! I see now what an ass I was not to wait and let you choose for yourself; these aesthetic things are not in my line. But I'd no idea you'd care so much!'

'But I don't now—a bit.'

'Well, I do, then. And the house must be done all over again, and exactly as you would like it; so there's no more to be said about it,' said George, without a trace of pique or wounded vanity.

'George, you are too good to me; I don't deserve it. And indeed you must not—think of the expense!'

His face lengthened slightly; he knew well enough that the change would cost him dear.

'I'll manage it somehow,' he declared stoutly.

Would her mother help them now? thought Ella, and felt more than doubtful. No, in spite of her own wishes, she must not allow George to carry out his intentions.

'But you forget Carrie and Jessie,' she said; 'we shall hurt their feelings so if we change now.'

'By Jove! I forgot that,' he said. 'Yes, they won't like it—they meant well, poor girls, and took a lot of trouble. Still, you're the first person to be considered, Ella. I'll try and smooth it over with them, and if they choose to be offended, why, they must—that's all. And I tell you what. Suppose we go and see the house now, and you shall tell me just what wants doing to make it right?'

She would have liked to decline this rather invidious office, especially as she felt no compromise to be possible; but he was so urgent that she finally agreed to go with him.

As they gained Campden Hill and the road in which their house stood, George stopped. 'Hullo!' he said, 'that can't be the house—what's the matter with it?'

Very soon it was pretty evident what had been the matter—the walls were scorched and streaming, the window sashes were empty, charred and wasted by fire, the door was blistered and blackened, a stalwart fireman in his undress cap, with his helmet slung at his back, was just opening the gate as they came up.

'Can't come in, sir,' he said, civilly enough. 'No one admitted.'

'Hang it!' exclaimed George, 'it's my own fire—I'm the tenant.'

'Oh, I beg your pardon, sir—it's been got under some hours now. I was just going off duty.'

'Much damage done?' inquired George laconically.

'Well, you see, sir,' said the man, evidently considering how to prepare George for the worst, 'we didn't get the call till the house was well alight, and there was three steamers and a manual a-playing on it, so—well, you must expect things to be a bit untidy-like inside. But the walls and the roof ain't much damaged.'

'And how did it happen?—the house isn't even occupied.'

'Workmen,' said the man. 'Someone was in there early this morning and left the gas escaping somewheres, and as likely as not a light burning near—and here you are. Well, I'll be off, sir; there's nothing more to be done 'ere. Good-day, sir, and thank ye, I'm sure.'

'Oh, George!' said Ella, half crying, 'our poor, poor little house! It seems like a judgment on me. How can you laugh! Who will build it up for us now?'

'Who? Why, the insurance people, to be sure! You see, the firm are agents for the "Curfew," and as soon as I got all the furniture in I insured the whole concern and got a protection note, so we're all right. Don't worry, little girl. Why, don't you see this gets us out of our difficulty? We can start afresh now without offending anybody. Look there; there's that idiot of a plumber who's done all the mischief—a nice funk he'll be in when he sees us!'

But Mr. Peagrum was quite unperturbed; if anything, his smudgy features wore a look of sombre complacency as he came towards them. 'I'm sorry this should have occurred,' he said,'but you'll bear me out that I warned yer as something was bound to 'appen. In course I couldn't tell what form it might take, and fire I must say I did not expect. I 'adn't on'y been in the place not a quarter of a hour, watering the gaselier in the libery—the libery as was, I should say—when it struck me I'd forgot my screw-driver, so, fortunately, as things turned out, I went 'ome to my place to get it, and I come back to see the place all in a blaze. It's fate, that's what it is—fate's at the bottom o' this 'ere job!'

'Much more likely to be a lighted candle,' said George.

'I was not on the premises at the time, so I can't say; but, be that 'ow it may, there's no denying it's a singler thing the way my words have been fulfilled almost literal.'

'Confound you!' said George. 'You take good care your prophecies come off. Why, man, you're not going to pretend you don't know that it's your own carelessness that's brought this about! This isn't the only house you've brought bad luck into, Mr. What's-your-name, since you've started in business!'

'You can't make me lose my temper,' replied the plumber with dignity. 'I put it down to ignirance.'

'So do I,' said George. 'And if I know anyone who's anxious for a little typhoid, or wants his house burnt down at a moderate charge, why, I shall know whom to recommend. Good-day.'

He turned on his heel and walked off, but Ella lingered behind. 'I only just wanted to tell you,' she said, addressing the astonished plumber, 'that you have done us a very great service, and I, at least, am very much obliged to you.' And she fluttered away after her fiance.

The plumber—that instrument of Destiny—looked after the retreating couple, and indulged in a mystified whistle.

"E comes a bullyragging of me,' he observed to a lamp-post, 'and she's "very much obliged"! And I'm blowed if I know what for, either way! Cracked, poor young things, cracked, the pair on 'em—and no wonder, with such a calamity so recent. Ah, well, I do 'ope as this is the end on it. I 'ope I shan't be the means of bringing no more trouble into that little 'ouse—that I kin truly say!'

And—human gratitude having its limits—it is highly probable that this pious aspiration will not be disappointed, so long, at least, as Mr. and Mrs. Chapman's tenancy continues.

The Siren

Long long ago, a siren lived all alone upon a rocky little island far out in the Southern Ocean. She may have been the youngest and most beautiful of the original three sirens, driven by her sisters' jealousy, or her own weariness of their society, to seek this distant home; or she may have lived there in solitude from the beginning.

But she was not unhappy; all she cared about was the admiration and worship of mortal men, and these were hers whenever she wished, for she had only to sing, and her exquisite voice would float away over the waters, until it reached some passing vessel, and then every one that heard was seized instantly with the irresistible longing to hasten to her isle and throw himself adoringly at her feet.

One day as she sat upon a low headland, looking earnestly out over the sparkling blue-green water before her, and hoping to discover the peak of some far-off sail on the hazy sea-line, she was startled by a sound she had never heard before—the grating of a boat's keel on the pebbles in the little creek at her side.

She had been too much absorbed in watching for distant ships to notice that a small bark had been gliding round the other side of her island, but now, as she glanced round, she saw that the stranger who had guided it was already jumping ashore and securing his boat.

Evidently she had not attracted him there, for she had been too indolent to sing of late, and he did not seem even to have seen her, or to have landed from any other motive than curiosity.

He was quite young, gallant-looking and sunburnt, with brown hair curling over his forehead, an open face and honest grey eyes. And as she looked at him, the fancy came to her that she would like to question him and hear his voice; she would find out, if she could, what manner of beings these mortals were over whom she possessed so strange a power.

Never before had such a thought entered her mind, notwithstanding that she had seen many mortals of every age and rank, from captain to the lowest galley slave; but then she had only seen them under the influence of her magical voice, when they were struck dumb and motionless, after which—except as proofs of her power—they did not interest her.

But this stranger was still free—so long as she did not choose to enslave him; and for some reason she did not choose to do so just yet.

As he turned towards her, she beckoned to him imperiously, and he saw the slender graceful figure above for the first time,—the fairest maiden his eyes had ever beheld, with an unearthly beauty in her wonderful dark blue eyes, and hair of the sunniest gold,—he stood gazing at her in motionless uncertainty, for he thought he must be cheated by a vision.

He came nearer, and, obeying a careless motion of her hand, threw himself down on a broad shelf of rock a little below the spot where she was seated; still he did not dare to speak lest the vision should pass away.

She looked at him for some time with an innocent, almost childish, curiosity shining under her long lashes. At last she gave a low little laugh: 'Are you afraid of me?' she asked; 'why don't you speak? but perhaps,' she added to herself, 'mortals cannot speak.'

'I was silent,' he said, 'lest by speaking I should anger you—for surely you must be some goddess or sea-nymph?'

'Ah, you can speak!' she cried. 'No, I am no goddess or nymph, and you will not anger me—if only you will tell me many things I want to know!'

And she began to ask him all the questions she could think of: first about the great world in which men lived, and then about himself, for she was very curious, in a charmingly wilful and capricious fashion of her own.

He answered frankly and simply, but it seemed as if some influence were upon him which kept him from being dazzled and overcome by her loveliness, for he gave no sign as yet of yielding to the glamour she cast upon all other men, nor did his eyes gleam with the despairing adoration the siren knew so well.

She was quick to perceive this, and it piqued her. She paid less and less attention to the answers he gave her, and ceased at last to question him further.

Presently she said, with a strange smile that showed her cruel little teeth gleaming between her scarlet lips, 'Why don't you ask me who I am, and what I am doing here alone? do not you care to know?'

'If you will deign to tell me,' he said.

'Then I will tell you,' she said; 'I am a siren—are you not afraid now?'

'Why should I be afraid?' he asked, for the name had no meaning in his ears.

She was disappointed; it was only her voice—nothing else, then—that deprived men of their senses; perhaps this youth was proof even against that; she longed to try, and yet she hesitated still.

'Then you have never heard of me,' she said; 'you don't know why I sit and watch for the great gilded ships you mortals build for yourselves?'

'For your pleasure, I suppose,' he answered. 'I have watched them myself many a time; they are grand as they sweep by, with their sharp brazen beaks cleaving the frothing water, and their painted sails curving out firm against the sky. It is good to hear the measured thud of the great oars and the cheerful cries of the sailors as they clamber about the cordage.'

She laughed disdainfully. 'And you think I care for all that!' she cried. 'Where is the pleasure of looking idly on and admiring?—that is for them, not for me. As these galleys of yours pass, I sing—and when the sailors hear, they must come to me. Man after man leaps eagerly into the sea, and makes for the shore—until at last the oars grind and lock together, and the great ship drifts helplessly on, empty and aimless. I like that.'

'But the men?' he asked, with an uneasy wonder at her words.

'Oh, they reach the shore—some of them, and then they lie at my feet, just as you are lying now, and I sing on, and as they listen they lose all power or wish to move, nor have I ever heard them speak as you speak; they only lie there upon the sand or rock, and gaze at me always, and soon their cheeks grow hollower and hollower, and their eyes brighter and brighter—and it is I who make them so!'

'But I see them not,' said the youth, divided between hope and fear; 'the beach is bare; where, then, are all those gone who have lain here?'

'I cannot say,' she replied carelessly; 'they are not here for long; when the sea comes up it carries them away.'

'And you do not care!' he cried, struck with horror at the absolute indifference in her face; 'you do not even try to keep them here?'

'Why should I care?' said the siren lightly; 'I do not want them. More will always come when I wish. And it is so wearisome always to see the same faces, that I am glad when they go.'

'I will not believe it, siren,' groaned the young man, turning from her in bitter anguish; 'oh, you cannot be cruel!'

'No, I am not cruel,' she said in surprise. 'And why will you not believe me? It is true!'

'Listen to me,' he said passionately: 'do you know how bitter it is to die,—to leave the sunlight and the warm air, the fair land and the changing sea?'

'How can I know?' said the siren. 'I shall never die—unless—unless something happens which will never be!'

'You will live on, to bring this bitterness upon others for your sport. We mortals lead but short lives, and life, even spent in sorrow, is sweet to most of us; and our deaths when they come bring mourning to those who cared for us and are left behind. But you lure men to this isle, and look on unmoved as they are borne away!'

'No, you are wrong,' she said; 'I am not cruel, as you think me; when they are no longer pleasant to look at, I leave them. I never see them borne away. I never thought what became of them at last. Where are they now?'

'They are dead, siren,' he said sadly, 'drowned. Life was dear to them; far away there were women and children to whom they had hoped to return, and who have waited and wept for them since. Happy years were before them, and to some at least—but for you—a restful and honoured old age. But you called them, and as they lay here the greedy waves came up, dashed them from these rocks and sucked them, blinded, suffocating, battling painfully for breath and life, down into the dark green depths. And now their bones lie tangled in the sea-weed, but they themselves are wandering, sad, restless shades, in the shadowy world below, where is no sun, no happiness, no hope—but only sighing evermore, and the memory of the past!'

She listened with drooping lids, and her chin resting upon her soft palm; at last she said with a slight quiver in her voice,'I did not know—I did not mean them to die. And what can I do? I cannot keep back the sea.'

'You can let them sail by unharmed,' he said.

'I cannot!' she cried. 'Of what use is my power to me if I may not exercise it? Why do you tell me of men's sufferings—what are they to me?'

'They give you their lives,' he said; 'you fill them with a hopeless love and they die for it in misery—yet you cannot even pity them!'

'Is it love that brings them here?' she said eagerly. 'What is this that is called love? For I have always known that if I ever love—but then only—I must die, though what love may be I know not. Tell me, so that I may avoid it!'

'You need not fear, siren,' he said, 'for, if death is only to come to you through love, you will never die!'

'Still, I want to know,' she insisted; 'tell me!'

'If a stranger were to come some day to this isle, and when his eyes meet yours, you feel your indifference leaving you, so that you have no heart to see him lie ignobly at your feet, and cannot leave him to perish miserably in the cold waters; if you desire to keep him by your side—not as your slave and victim, but as your companion, your equal, for evermore—that will be love!'

'If that is love,' she cried joyously, 'I shall indeed never die! But that is not how men love me?' she added.

'No,' he said; 'their love for you must be some strange and enslaving passion, since they will submit to death if only they may hear your voice. That is not true love, but a fatal madness.'

'But if mortals feel love for one another,' she asked,'they must die, must they not?'

'The love of a man for a maiden who is gentle and good does not kill—even when it is most hopeless,' he said; 'and where she feels it in return, it is well for both, for their lives will flow on together in peace and happiness.'

He had spoken softly, with a far away look in his eyes that did not escape the siren.

'And you love one of your mortal maidens like that?' she asked. 'Is she more beautiful than I am?'

'She is mortal,' he said, 'but she is fair and gracious, my maiden; and it is she who has my love, and will have it while I live.'

'And yet,' she said, with a mocking smile, 'I could make you forget her.'

Her childlike waywardness had left her as she spoke the words, and a dangerous fire was shining in her deep eyes.

'Never!' he cried; 'even you cannot make me false to my love! And yet,' he added quickly, 'I dare not challenge you, enchantress that you are; what is my will against your power?'

'You do not love me yet,' she said; 'you have called me cruel, and reproached me; you have dared to tell me of a maiden compared with whom I am nothing! You shall be punished. I will have you for my own, like the others!'

'Siren,' he pleaded, seizing one of her hands as it lay close to him on the hot grey rock, 'take my life if you will—but do not drive away the memory of my love; let me die, if I must die, faithful to her; for what am I, or what is my love, to you?'

'Nothing,' she said scornfully, and yet with something of a caress in her tone, 'yet I want you; you shall lie here, and hold my hand, and look into my eyes, and forget all else but me.'

'Let me go,' he cried, rising, and turning back to regain his bark; 'I choose life while I may!'

She laughed. 'You have no choice,' she said; 'you are mine!' she seemed to have grown still more radiantly, dazzlingly fair, and presently, as the stranger made his way to the creek where his boat was lying, she broke into the low soft chant whose subtle witchery no mortals had ever resisted as yet.

He started as he heard her, but still he went on over the rocks a little longer, until at last he stopped with a groan, and turned slowly back; his love across the sea was fading fast from his memory; he felt no desire to escape any longer; he was even eager at last to be back on the ledge at her feet and listen to her for ever.

He reached it and sank down with a sigh, and a drowsy delicious languor stole over him, taking away all power to stir or speak.

Her song was triumphant and mocking, and yet strangely tender at times, thrilling him as he heard it, but her eyes only rested now and then, and always indifferently, upon his upturned face.

He wished for nothing better now than to lie there, following the flashing of her supple hands upon the harp-strings and watching every change of her fair face. What though the waves might rise round him and sweep him away out of sight, and drown her voice with the roar and swirl of waters? it would not be just yet.

And the siren sang on; at first with a cruel pride at finding her power supreme, and this youth, for all his fidelity, no wiser than the rest; he would waste there with yearning, hopeless passion, till the sight of him would weary her, and she would leave him to drift away and drown forgotten.

Yet she did not despise him as she had despised all the others; in her fancy his eyes bore a sad reproach, and she could look at him no longer with indifference.

Meanwhile the waves came rolling in fast, till they licked the foot of the rock, and as the foam creamed over the shingle, the siren found herself thinking of the fate which was before him, and, as she thought, her heart was wrung with a new strange pity.

She did not want him to be drowned; she would like him there always at her feet, with that rapt devotion upon his face; she almost longed to hear his voice again—but that could never be!

And the sun went down, and the crimson flush in the sky and on the sea faded out, the sea grew grey and crested with the white billows, which came racing in and broke upon the shore, roaring sullenly and raking back the pebbles with a sharp rattle at each recoil. The siren could sing no longer; her voice died away, and she gazed on the troubled sea with a wistful sadness in her great eyes.

At last a wave larger than the others struck the face of the low cliff with a shock that seemed to leave it trembling, and sent the cold salt spray dashing up into the siren's face.

She sprang forward to the edge and looked over, with a sudden terror lest the ledge below should be bare—but her victim lay there still, bound fast by her spell, and careless of the death that was advancing upon him.

Then she knew for the first time that she could not give him up to the sea, and she leaned down to him and laid one small white hand upon his shoulder. 'The next wave will carry you away,' she cried, trembling; 'there is still time; save yourself, for I cannot let you die!'

But he gave no sign of having heard her, but lay there motionless, and the wind wailed past them and the sea grew wilder and louder.

She remembered now that no efforts of his own could save him—he was doomed, and she was the cause of it, and she hid her face in her slender hands, weeping for the first time in her life.

The words he had spoken in answer to her questions about love came back to her: 'It was true, then,' she said to herself; 'it is love that I feel for him. But I cannot love—I must not love him—for if I do, my power is gone, and I must throw myself into the sea!'

So she hardened her heart once more, and turned away, for she feared to die; but again the ground shook beneath her, and the spray rose high into the air, and then she could bear it no more—whatever it cost her, she must save him—for if he died, what good would her life be to her?

'If one of us must die,' she said, 'I will be that one. I am cruel and wicked, as he told me; I have done harm enough!' and bending down, she wound her arms round his unconscious body and drew him gently up to the level above.

'You are safe now,' she whispered; 'you shall not be drowned—for I love you. Sail back to your maiden on the mainland, and be happy; but do not hate me for the evil I have wrought, for suffering and death have come to me in my turn!'

The lethargy into which he had fallen left him under her clinging embrace, and the sad, tender words fell almost unconsciously upon his dulled ears; he felt the touch of her hair as it brushed his cheek, and his forehead was still warm with the kiss she had pressed there as he opened his eyes—only to find himself alone.

For the fate which the siren had dreaded had come upon her at last; she had loved, and she had paid the penalty for loving, and never more would her wild, sweet voice beguile mortals to their doom.

The Black Poodle

I have set myself the task of relating in the course of this story, without suppressing or altering a single detail, the most painful and humiliating episode of my life.

I do this, not because it will give me the least pleasure, but simply because it affords me an opportunity of extenuating myself, which has hitherto been wholly denied to me.

As a general rule, I am quite aware that to publish a lengthy explanation of one's conduct in any questionable transaction is not the best means of recovering a lost reputation; but in my own case there is one to whom I shall nevermore be permitted to justify by word of mouth—even if I found myself able to attempt it. And as she could not possibly think worse of me than she does at present, I write this, knowing it can do me no harm, and faintly hoping that it may come to her notice and suggest a doubt whether I am quite so unscrupulous a villain, so consummate a hypocrite, as I have been forced to appear in her eyes.

The bare chance of such a result makes me perfectly indifferent to all else; I cheerfully expose to the derision of the whole reading world the story of my weakness and my shame, since by doing so I may possibly rehabilitate myself somewhat in the good opinion of one person.

Having said so much, I will begin my confession without further delay.

My name is Algernon Weatherhead, and I may add that I am in one of the government departments, that I am an only son, and live at home with my mother.

We had had a house at Hammersmith until just before the period covered by this history, when, our lease expiring, my mother decided that my health required country air at the close of the day, and so we took a "desirable villa residence" on one of the many new building estates which have lately sprung up in such profusion in the home counties.

We have called it "Wistaria Villa." It is a pretty little place, the last of a row of detached villas, each with its tiny rustic carriage-gate and gravel sweep in front, and lawn enough for a tennis-court behind, which lines the road leading over the hill to the railway-station.

I could certainly have wished that our landlord, shortly after giving us the agreement, could have found some other place to hang himself in than one of our attics, for the consequence was that a housemaid left us in violent hysterics about every two months, having learned the tragedy from the tradespeople, and naturally "seen a somethink" immediately afterward.

Still it is a pleasant house, and I can now almost forgive the landlord for what I shall always consider an act of gross selfishness on his part.

In the country, even so near town, a next-door neighbor is something more than a mere numeral; he is a possible acquaintance, who will at least consider a new-comer as worth the experiment of a call. I soon knew that "Shuturgarden," the next house to our own, was occupied by a Colonel Currie, a retired Indian officer; and often, as across the low boundary wall I caught a glimpse of a graceful girlish figure flitting about among the rose-bushes in the neighbouring garden, I would lose myself in pleasant anticipations of a time not too far distant when the wall which separated us would be (metaphorically) levelled.

I remember—ah, how vividly!—the thrill of excitement with which I heard from my mother, on returning from town one evening, that the Curries had called, and seemed disposed to be all that was neighbourly and kind.

I remember, too, the Sunday afternoon on which I returned their call—alone, as my mother had already done so during the week. I was standing on the steps of the colonel's villa, waiting for the door to open, when I was startled by a furious snarling and yapping behind, and, looking round, discovered a large poodle in the act of making for my legs.

He was a coal-black poodle, with half of his right ear gone, and absurd little thick moustaches at the end of his nose; he was shaved in the shamlion fashion, which is considered, for some mysterious reason, to improve a poodle, but the barber had left sundry little tufts of hair, which studded his haunches capriciously.

I could not help being reminded, as I looked at him, of another black poodle, which Faust entertained for a short time with unhappy results, and I thought that a very moderate degree of incantation would be enough to bring the fiend out of this brute.

He made me intensely uncomfortable, for I am of a slightly nervous temperament, with a constitutional horror of dogs, and a liability to attacks of diffidence on performing the ordinary social rites under the most favourable conditions, and certainly the consciousness that a strange and apparently savage dog was engaged in worrying the heels of my boots was the reverse of reassuring.

The Currie family received me with all possible kindness. "So charmed to make your acquaintance, Mr. Weatherhead," said Mrs. Currie, as I shook hands. "I see," she added, pleasantly, "you've brought the doggie in with you." As a matter of fact, I had brought the doggie in at the ends of my coat-tails; but it was evidently no unusual occurrence for visitors to appear in this undignified manner, for she detached him quite as a matter of course, and as soon as I was sufficiently collected we fell into conversation.

I discovered that the colonel and his wife were childless, and the slender willowy figure I had seen across the garden wall was that of Lilian Roseblade, their niece and adopted daughter. She came into the room shortly afterward, and I felt, as I went through the form of an introduction, that her sweet, fresh face, shaded by soft masses of dusky-brown hair, more than justified all the dreamy hopes and fancies with which I had looked forward to that moment.

She talked to me in a pretty, confidential, appealing way, which I have heard her dearest friends censure as childish and affected; but I thought then that her manner had an indescribable charm and fascination about it, and the memory of it makes my heart ache now with a pang that is not all pain.

Even before the colonel made his appearance I had begun to see that my enemy, the poodle, occupied an exceptional position in that household. It was abundantly clear by the time I took my leave.

He seemed to be the centre of their domestic system, and even lovely Lilian revolved contentedly around him as a kind of satellite; he could do no wrong in his owner's eyes, his prejudices (and he was a narrow-minded animal) were rigorously respected, and all domestic arrangements were made with a primary view to his convenience.

I may be wrong, but I cannot think that it is wise to put any poodle upon such a pedestal as that. How this one in particular, as ordinary a quadruped as ever breathed, had contrived to impose thus upon his infatuated proprietors, I never could understand, but so it was; he even engrossed the chief part of the conversation, which after any lull seemed to veer round to him by a sort of natural law.

I had to endure a long biographical sketch of him,—what a society paper would call an "anecdotal photo,"—and each fresh anecdote seemed to me to exhibit the depraved malignity of the beast in a more glaring light, and render the doting admiration of the family more astounding than ever.

"Did you tell Mr. Weatherhead, Lily, about Bingo" (Bingo was the poodle's preposterous name) "and Tacks? No? Oh, I must tell him that; it'll make him laugh. Tacks is our gardener down in the village (d' ye know Tacks?). Well, Tacks was up here the other day, nailing up some trellis-work at the top of a ladder, and all the time there was Master Bingo sitting quietly at the foot of it looking on; wouldn't leave it on any account. Tacks said he was quite company for him. Well, at last, when Tacks had finished and was coming down, what do you thing that rascal there did? Just sneaked quietly up behind and nipped him in both calves and ran off. Been looking out for that the whole time! Ha, ha!—deep that, eh?"

I agreed, with an inward shudder, that it was very deep, thinking privately that, if this was a specimen of Bingo's usual treatment of the natives, it would be odd if he did not find himself deeper still before— probably just before—he died.

"Poor, faithful old doggie!" murmured Mrs. Currie; "he thought Tacks was a nasty burglar, didn't he? He wasn't going to see master robbed was he?"

"Capital house-dog, sir," struck in the colonel. "Gad, I shall never forget how he made poor Heavisides run for it the other day! Ever met Heavisides of the Bombay Fusileers? Well, Heavisides was staying here, and the dog met him one morning as he was coming down from the bath-room. Didn't recognise him in 'pajamas' and a dressing-gown, of course, and made at him. He kept poor old Heavisides outside the landing window on top of the cistern for a quarter of an hour, till I had to come and raise the siege!"

Such were the stories of that abandoned dog's blunderheaded ferocity to which I was forced to listen, while all the time the brute sat opposite me on the hearth-rug, blinking at me from under his shaggy mane with his evil, bleared eyes, and deliberating where he would have me when I rose to go.

This was the beginning of an intimacy which soon displaced all ceremony. It was very pleasant to go in there after dinner, even to sit with the colonel over his claret, and hear more stories about Bingo; for afterward I could go into the pretty drawing-room and take my tea from Lilian's hands, and listen while she played Schubert to us in the summer twilight.

The poodle was always in the way, to be sure, but even his ugly black head seemed to lose some of its ugliness and ferocity when Lilian laid her pretty hand on it.

On the whole, I think that the Currie family were well disposed toward me, the colonel considering me as a harmless specimen of the average eligible young man,—which I certainly was,—and Mrs. Currie showing me favour for my mother's sake, for whom she had taken a strong liking.

As for Lilian, I believed I saw that she soon suspected the state of my feelings toward her, and was not displeased by it. I looked forward with some hopefulness to a day when I could declare myself with no fear of a repulse.

But it was a serious obstacle in my path that I could not secure Bingo's good opinion on any terms. The family would often lament this pathetically themselves. "You see," Mrs. Currie would observe in apology, "Bingo is a dog that does not attach himself easily to strangers"—though, for that matter, I thought he was unpleasantly ready to attach himself to me.

I did try hard to conciliate him. I brought him propitiatory buns, which was weak and ineffectual, as he ate them with avidity, and hated me as bitterly as ever; for he had conceived from the first a profound contempt for me, and a distrust which no blandishments of mine could remove. Looking back now, I am inclined to think it was a prophetic instinct that warned him of what was to come upon him through my instrumentality.

Only his approbation was wanting to establish for me a firm footing with the Curries, and perhaps determine Lilian's wavering heart in my direction; but, though I wooed that inflexible poodle with an assiduity I blush to remember, he remained obstinately firm.

Still, day by day, Lilian's treatment of me was more encouraging; day by day I gained in the esteem of her uncle and aunt; I began to hope that soon I should be able to disregard canine influence altogether.

Now there was one inconvenience about our villa (besides its flavour of suicide) which it is necessary to mention here. By common consent all the cats of the neighbourhood had selected our garden for their evening reunions. I fancy that a tortoise-shell kitchen cat of ours must have been a sort of leader of local feline society—I know she was "at home," with music and recitations, on most evenings.

My poor mother found this to interfere with her after-dinner nap, and no wonder; for if a cohort of ghosts had been "shrieking and squealing," as Calpurnia puts it, in our back garden, or it had been fitted up as a creche for a nursery of goblin infants in the agonies of teething, the noise could not possibly have been more unearthly.

We sought for some means of getting rid of the nuisance: there was poison, of course; but we thought it would have an invidious appearance, and even lead to legal difficulties, if each dawn were to discover an assortment of cats expiring in hideous convulsions in various parts of the same garden.

Firearms too were open to objection, and would scarcely assist my mother's slumbers; so for some time we were at a loss for a remedy. At last, one day, walking down the Strand, I chanced to see (in an evil hour) what struck me as the very thing: it was an air-gun of superior construction, displayed in a gunsmith's window. I went in at once, purchased it, and took it home in triumph; it would be noiseless, and would reduce the local average of cats without scandal,—one or two examples,—and feline fashion would soon migrate to a more secluded spot.

I lost no time in putting this to the proof. That same evening I lay in wait after dusk at the study window, protecting my mother's repose. As soon as I heard the long-drawn wail, the preliminary sputter, and the wild stampede that followed, I let fly in the direction of the sound. I suppose I must have something of the national sporting instinct in me, for my blood was tingling with excitement; but the feline constitution assimilates lead without serious inconvenience, and I began to fear that no trophy would remain to bear witness to my marksmanship.

But all at once I made out a dark, indistinct form slinking in from behind the bushes. I waited till it crossed a belt of light which streamed from the back kitchen below me, and then I took careful aim and pulled the trigger.

This time at least I had not failed; there was a smothered yell, a rustle, and then silence again. I ran out with the calm pride of a successful revenge to bring in the body of my victim, and I found underneath a laurel no predatory tom-cat, but (as the discerning reader will no doubt have foreseen long since) the quivering carcass of the colonel's black poodle!

I intend to set down here the exact unvarnished truth, and I confess that at first, when I knew what I had done, I was not sorry. I was quite innocent of any intention of doing it, but I felt no regret. I even laughed—madman that I was—at the thought that there was the end of Bingo, at all events; that impediment was removed; my weary task of conciliation was over for ever!

But soon the reaction came; I realised the tremendous nature of my deed, and shuddered. I had done that which might banish me from Lilian's side for ever! All unwittingly I had slaughtered a kind of sacred beast, the animal around which the Currie household had wreathed their choicest affections! How was I to break it to them? Should I send Bingo in, with a card tied to his neck and my regrets and compliments? That was too much like a present of game. Ought I not to carry him in myself? I would wreathe him in the best crape, I would put on black for him; the Curries would hardly consider a taper and a white sheet, or sack-cloth and ashes, an excessive form of atonement, but I could not grovel to quite such an abject extent.

I wondered what the colonel would say. Simple and hearty, as a general rule, he had a hot temper on occasions, and it made me ill as I thought, would he and, worse still, would Lilian believe it was really an accident? They knew what an interest I had in silencing the deceased poodle—would they believe the simple truth?

I vowed that they should believe me. My genuine remorse and the absence of all concealment on my part would speak powerfully for me. I would choose a favourable time for my confession; that very evening I would tell all.

Still I shrank from the duty before me, and, as I knelt down sorrowfully by the dead form and respectfully composed his stiffening limbs, I thought that it was unjust of fate to place a well-meaning man, whose nerves were not of iron, in such a position.

Then, to my horror, I heard a well-known ringing tramp on the road outside, and smelled the peculiar fragrance of a Burmese cheroot. It was the colonel himself, who had been taking out the doomed Bingo for his usual evening run.

I don't know how it was, exactly, but a sudden panic came over me. I held my breath, and tried to crouch down unseen behind the laurels; but he had seen me, and came over at once to speak to me across the hedge.

He stood there, not two yards from his favourite's body! Fortunately it was unusually dark that evening.

"Ha, there you are, eh!" he began, heartily; "don't rise, my boy, don't rise."

I was trying to put myself in front of the poodle, and did not rise—at least, only my hair did.

"You're out late, ain't you?" he went on; "laying out your garden, hey?"

I could not tell him that I was laying out his poodle! My voice shook as, with a guilty confusion that was veiled by the dusk, I said it was a fine evening—which it was not.

"Cloudy, sir," said the colonel, "cloudy; rain before morning, I think. By the way, have you seen anything of Bingo in here?"

This was the turning-point. What I ought to have done was to say mournfully, "Yes, I'm sorry to say I've had a most unfortunate accident with him. Here he is; the fact is, I'm afraid I've shot him!"

But I couldn't. I could have told him at my own time, in a prepared form of words—but not then. I felt I must use all my wits to gain time, and fence with the questions.

"Why," I said, with a leaden airiness, "he hasn't given you the slip, has he?"

"Never did such a thing in his life!" said the colonel, warmly; "he rushed off after a rat or a frog or something a few minutes ago, and as I stopped to light another cheroot I lost sight of him. I thought I saw him slip in under your gate, but I've been calling him from the front there and he won't come out."

No, and he never would come out any more. But the colonel must not be told that just yet. I temporised again: "If," I said, unsteadily—"if he had slipped in under the gate I should have seen him. Perhaps he took it into his head to run home?"

"Oh, I shall find him on the door-step, I expect, the knowing old scamp! Why, what d' ye think was the last thing he did, now?"

I could have given him the very latest intelligence, but I dared not. However, it was altogether too ghastly to kneel there and laugh at anecdotes of Bingo told across Bingo's dead body; I could not stand that. "Listen," I said, suddenly, "wasn't that his bark? There, again; it seems to come from the front of your house, don't you think?"

"Well," said the colonel, "I'll go and fasten him up before he's off again. How your teeth are chattering! You've caught a chill, man; go indoors at once, and, if you feel equal to it, look in half an hour later, about grog-time, and I'll tell you all about it. Compliments to your mother. Don't forget—about grog-time!"

I had got rid of him at last, and I wiped my forehead, gasping with relief. I would go round in half an hour, and then I should be prepared to make my melancholy announcement. For, even then, I never thought of any other course, until suddenly it flashed upon me with terrible clearness that my miserable shuffling by the hedge had made it impossible to tell the truth! I had not told a direct lie, to be sure, but then I had given the colonel the impression that I had denied having seen the dog. Many people can appease their consciences by reflecting that, whatever may be the effect their words produce, they did contrive to steer clear of a downright lie. I never quite knew where the distinction lay morally, but there is that feeling—I have it myself.

Unfortunately, prevarication has this drawback: that, if ever the truth comes to light, the prevaricator is in just the same case as if he had lied to the most shameless extent, and for a man to point out that the words he used contained no absolute falsehood will seldom restore confidence.

I might, of course, still tell the colonel of my misfortune, and leave him to infer that it had happened after our interview; but the poodle was fast becoming cold and stiff, and they would most probably suspect the real time of the occurrence.

And then Lilian would hear that I had told a string of falsehoods to her uncle over the dead body of their idolised Bingo—an act, no doubt, of abominable desecration, of unspeakable profanity, in her eyes.

If it would have been difficult before to prevail on her to accept a blood-stained hand, it would be impossible after that. No, I had burned my ships, I was cut off for ever from the straightforward course; that one moment of indecision had decided my conduct in spite of me; I must go on with it now, and keep up the deception at all hazards.

It was bitter. I had always tried to preserve as many of the moral principles which had been instilled into me as can be conveniently retained in this grasping world, and it had been my pride that, roughly speaking, I had never been guilty of an unmistakable falsehood.

But henceforth, if I meant to win Lilian, that boast must be relinquished for ever. I should have to lie now with all my might, without limit or scruple, to dissemble incessantly, and "wear a mask," as the poet

Bunn beautifully expressed it long ago, "over my hollow heart." I felt all this keenly; I did not think it was right, but what was I to do?

After thinking all this out very carefully, I decided that my only course was to bury the poor animal where he fell, and say nothing about it. With some vague idea of precaution, I first took off the silver collar he wore, and then hastily interred him with a garden-trowel, and succeeded in removing all traces of the disaster.

I fancy I felt a certain relief in the knowledge that there would now be no necessity to tell my pitiful story and risk the loss of my neighbours' esteem.

By-and-by, I thought, I would plant a rose-tree over his remains, and some day, as Lilian and I, in the noontide of our domestic bliss, stood before it admiring its creamy luxuriance, I might (perhaps) find courage to confess that the tree owed some of that luxuriance to the long-lost Bingo.

There was a touch of poetry in this idea that lightened my gloom for the moment.

I need scarcely say that I did not go round to Shuturgarden that evening. I was not hardened enough for that yet; my manner might betray me, and so I very prudently stayed at home.

But that night my sleep was broken by frightful dreams. I was perpetually trying to bury a great, gaunt poodle, which would persist in rising up through the damp mould as fast as I covered him up. . . . Lilian and I were engaged, and we were in church together on Sunday, and the poodle, resisting all attempts to eject him, forbade our banns with sepulchral barks. . . . It was our wedding-day, and at the critical moment the poodle leaped between us and swallowed the ring. . . . Or we were at the wedding-breakfast, and Bingo, a grisly black skeleton with flaming eyes, sat on the cake and would not allow Lilian to cut it. Even the rose-tree fancy was reproduced in a distorted form—the tree grew, and every blossom contained a miniature Bingo, which barked; and as I woke I was desperately trying to persuade the colonel that they were ordinary dog-roses.

I went up to the office next day with my gloomy secret gnawing my bosom, and, whatever I did, the spectre of the murdered poodle rose before me. For two days after that I dared not go near the Curries, until at last one evening after dinner I forced myself to call, feeling that it was really not safe to keep away any longer.

My conscience smote me as I went in. I put on an unconscious, easy manner, which was such a dismal failure that it was lucky for me that they were too much engrossed to notice it.

I never before saw a family so stricken down by a domestic misfortune as the group I found in the drawing-room, making a dejected pretence of reading or working. We talked at first—and hollow talk it was—on indifferent subjects, till I could bear it no longer, and plunged boldly into danger.

"I don't see the dog," I began, "I suppose you—you found him all right the other evening, colonel?" I wondered, as I spoke, whether they would not notice the break in my voice, but they did not.

"Why, the fact is," said the colonel, heavily, gnawing his gray moustache, "we've not heard anything of him since; he's—he's run off!"

"Gone, Mr. Weatherhead; gone without a word!" said Mrs. Currie, plaintively, as if she thought the dog might at least have left an address.

"I wouldn't have believed it of him," said the colonel; "it has completely knocked me over. Haven't been so cut up for years—the ungrateful rascal!"

"O uncle!" pleaded Lilian, "don't talk like that; perhaps Bingo couldn't help it—perhaps some one has s-s-shot him!"

"Shot!" cried the colonel, angrily. "By heaven! if I thought there was a villain on earth capable of shooting that poor inoffensive dog, I'd—Why should they shoot him, Lilian? Tell me that! I—I hope you won't let me hear you talk like that again. You don't think he's shot, eh, Weatherhead?"

I said—Heaven forgive me!—that I thought it highly improbable.

"He's not dead!" cried Mrs. Currie. "If he were dead I should know it somehow—I'm sure I should! But I'm certain he's alive. Only last night I had such a beautiful dream about him. I thought he came back to us, Mr. Weatherhead, driving up in a hansom-cab, and he was just the same as ever—only he wore blue spectacles, and the shaved part of him was painted a bright red. And I woke up with the joy—so, you know, it's sure to come true!"

It will be easily understood what torture conversations like these were to me, and how I hated myself as I sympathised and spoke encouraging words concerning the dog's recovery, when I knew all the time he was lying hid under my garden mould. But I took it as a part of my punishment, and bore it all uncomplainingly; practice even made me an adept in the art of consolation—I believe I really was a great comfort to them.

I had hoped that they would soon get over the first bitterness of their loss, and that Bingo would be first replaced and then forgotten in the usual way; but there seemed no signs of this coming to pass.

The poor colonel was too plainly fretting himself ill about it; he went pottering about forlornly, advertising, searching, and seeing people, but all, of course, to no purpose; and it told upon him. He was more like a man whose only son and heir had been stolen than an Anglo-Indian officer who had lost a poodle. I had to affect the liveliest interest in all his inquiries and expeditions, and to listen to and echo the most extravagant eulogies of the departed; and the wear and tear of so much duplicity made me at last almost as ill as the colonel himself.

I could not help seeing that Lilian was not nearly so much impressed by my elaborate concern as her relatives, and sometimes I detected an incredulous look in her frank brown eyes that made me very uneasy. Little by little, a rift widened between us, until at last in despair I determined to know the worst before the time came when it would be hopeless to speak at all. I chose a Sunday evening as we were walking across the green from church in the golden dusk, and then I ventured to speak to her of my love. She heard me to the end, and was evidently very much agitated. At last she murmured that it could not be, unless—no, it never could be now.

"Unless, what?" I asked. "Lilian—Miss Roseblade, something has come between us lately; you will tell me what that something is, won't you?"

"Do you want to know really?" she said, looking up at me through her tears. "Then I'll tell you; it—it's Bingo!"

I started back overwhelmed. Did she know all? If not, how much did she suspect? I must find out that at once. "What about Bingo?" I managed to pronounce, with a dry tongue.

"You never l-loved him when he was here," she sobbed; "you know you didn't!"

I was relieved to find it was no worse than this.

"No," I said, candidly; "I did not love Bingo. Bingo didn't love me, Lilian; he was always looking out for a chance of nipping me somewhere. Surely you won't quarrel with me for that!"

"Not for that," she said; "only, why do you pretend to be so fond of him now, and so anxious to get him back again? Uncle John believes you, but I don't. I can see quite well that you wouldn't be glad to find him. You could find him easily if you wanted to!"

"What do you mean, Lilian?" I said, hoarsely. "How could I find him?" Again I feared the worst.

"You're in a government office," cried Lilian, "and if you only chose, you could easily g-get g-government to find Bingo! What's the use of government if it can't do that? Mr. Travers would have found him long ago if I'd asked him!"

Lilian had never been so childishly unreasonable as this before, and yet I loved her more madly than ever; but I did not like this allusion to Travers, a rising barrister, who lived with his sister in a pretty cottage near the station, and had shown symptoms of being attracted by Lilian.

He was away on circuit just then, luckily; but, at least, even he would have found it a hard task to find Bingo—there was comfort in that.

"You know that isn't just, Lilian," I observed; "but only tell me what you want me to do."

"Bub-bub-bring back Bingo!" she said.

"Bring back Bingo!" I cried, in horror. "But suppose I can't—suppose he's out of the country, or—dead, what then Lilian?"

"I can't help it," she said, "but I don't believe he is out of the country or dead. And while I see you pretending to uncle that you cared awfully about him, and going on doing nothing at all, it makes me think you're not quite—quite sincere! And I couldn't possibly marry any one while I thought that of him. And I shall always have that feeling unless you find Bingo!"

It was of no use to argue with her; I knew Lilian by that time. With her pretty, caressing manner she united a latent obstinacy which it was hopeless to attempt to shake. I feared, too, that she was not quite certain as yet whether she cared for me or not, and that this condition of hers was an expedient to gain time.

I left her with a heavy heart. Unless I proved my worth by bringing back Bingo within a very short time, Travers would probably have everything his own way. And Bingo was dead!

However, I took heart. I thought that perhaps if I could succeed by my earnest efforts in persuading Lilian that I really was doing all in my power to recover the poodle, she might relent in time, and dispense with his actual production.

So, partly with this object, and partly to appease the remorse which now revived and stung me deeper than before, I undertook long and weary pilgrimages after office hours. I spent many pounds in advertisements; I interviewed dogs of every size, colour, and breed, and of course I took care to keep Lilian informed of each successive failure. But still her heart was not touched; she was firm. If I went on like that, she told me, I was certain to find Bingo one day; then, but not before, would her doubts be set at rest.

I was walking one day through the somewhat squalid district which lies between Bow Street and High Holborn, when I saw, in a small theatrical costumer's window, a hand-bill stating that a black poodle had "followed a gentleman" on a certain date, and if not claimed and the finder remunerated before a stated time would be sold to pay expenses.

I went in and got a copy of the bill to show Lilian, and, although by that time I scarcely dared to look a poodle in the face, I thought I would go to the address given and see the animal, simply to be able to tell Lilian I had done so.

The gentleman whom the dog had very unaccountably followed was a certain Mr. William Blagg, who kept a little shop near Endell Street, and called himself a bird-fancier, though I should scarcely have credited him with the necessary imagination. He was an evil-browed ruffian in a fur cap, with a broad broken nose and little shifty red eyes; and after I had told him what I wanted he took me through a horrible little den, stacked with piles of wooden, wire, and wicker prisons, each quivering with restless, twittering life, and then out into a back yard, in which were two or three rotten old kennels and tubs. "That there's him," he said, jerking his thumb to the farthest tub; "follered me all the way 'ome from Kinsington Gardens, he did. Kim out, will yer?"

And out of the tub there crawled slowly, with a snuffling whimper and a rattling of its chain, the identical dog I had slain a few evenings before!

At least, so I thought for a moment, and felt as if I had seen a spectre; the resemblance was so exact—in size, in every detail, even to the little clumps of hair about the hind parts, even to the lop of half an ear, this dog might have been the doppelganger of the deceased Bingo. I suppose, after all, one black poodle is very like any other black poodle of the same size, but the likeness startled me.

I think it was then that the idea occurred to me that here was a miraculous chance of securing the sweetest girl in the whole world, and at the same time atoning for my wrong by bringing back gladness with me to Shuturgarden. It only needed a little boldness; one last deception, and I could embrace truthfulness once more.

Almost unconsciously, when my guide turned round and asked, "Is that there dawg yourn?" I said hurriedly, "Yes, yes; that's the dog I want; that—that's Bingo!"

"He don't seem to be a-puttin' of 'isself out about seein' you again," observed Mr. Blagg, as the poodle studied me with calm interest.

"Oh, he's not exactly my dog, you see," I said; "he belongs to a friend of mine!"

He gave me a quick, furtive glance. "Then maybe you're mistook about him," he said, "and I can't run no risks. I was a-goin' down in the country this 'ere werry evenin' to see a party as lives at Wistaria Willa; he's been a-hadwertisin' about a black poodle, he has!"

"But look here," I said; "that's me."

He gave me a curious leer. "No offence, you know, guv'nor," he said, "but I should wish for some evidence as to that afore I part with a vallyable dawg like this 'ere!"

"Well," I said, "here's one of my cards; will that do for you?"

He took it and spelled it out with a pretence of great caution; but I saw well enough that the old schoundrel suspected that if I had lost a dog at all it was not this particular dog. "Ah," he said, as he put it in his pocket, "if I part with him to you I must be cleared of all risks. I can't afford to get into trouble about no mistakes. Unless you likes to leave him for a day or two you must pay accordin', you see."

I wanted to get the hateful business over as soon as possible. I did not care what I paid—Lilian was worth all the expense! I said I had no doubt myself as to the real ownership of the animal, but I would give him any sum in reason, and would remove the dog at once.

And so we settled it. I paid him an extortionate sum, and came away with a duplicate poodle, a canine counterfeit, which I hoped to pass off at Shuturgarden as the long-lost Bingo.

I know it was wrong,—it even came unpleasantly near dog-stealing,—but I was a desperate man. I saw Lilian gradually slipping away from me, I knew that nothing short of this could ever recall her, I was sorely tempted, I had gone far on the same road already; it was the old story of being hung for a sheep. And so I fell.

Surely some who read this will be generous enough to consider the peculiar state of the case, and mingle a little pity with their contempt.

I was dining in town that evening, and took my purchase home by a late train; his demeanour was grave and intensely respectable; he was not the animal to commit himself by any flagrant indiscretion; he was gentle and tractable too, and in all respects an agreeable contrast in character to the original. Still, it may have been the after-dinner workings of conscience, but I could not help fancying that I saw a certain look in the creature's eyes, as if he were aware that he was required to connive at a fraud, and rather resented it.

If he would only be good enough to back me up! Fortunately, however, he was such a perfect facsimile of the outward Bingo that the risk of detection was really inconsiderable.

When I got him home I put Bingo's silver collar round his neck, congratulating myself on my forethought in preserving it, and took him in to see my mother. She accepted him as what he seemed without the slightest misgiving; but this, though it encouraged me to go on, was not decisive—the spurious poodle would have to encounter the scrutiny of those who knew every tuft on the genuine animal's body!

Nothing would have induced me to undergo such an ordeal as that of personally restoring him to the Curries. We gave him supper, and tied him up on the lawn, where he howled dolefully all night and buried bones.

The next morning I wrote a note to Mrs. Currie, expressing my pleasure at being able to restore the lost one, and another to Lilian, containing only the words, "Will you believe now that I am sincere?" Then I tied both round the poodle's neck, and dropped him over the wall into the colonel's garden just before I started to catch my train to town.

I had an anxious walk home from the station that evening; I went round by the longer way, trembling the whole time lest I should meet any of the Currie household, to which I felt myself entirely unequal just then. I could not rest until I knew whether my fraud had succeeded, or if the poodle to which I had intrusted my fate had basely betrayed me; but my suspense was happily ended as soon as I entered my mother's room. "You can't think how delighted those poor Curries were to see Bingo again," she said at once; "and they said such charming things about you, Algy—Lilian particularly; quite affected she seemed, poor child! And they wanted you to go round and dine there and be thanked to-night, but at last I persuaded them to come to us instead. And they're going to bring the dog to make friends. Oh, and I met Frank Travers; he's back from circuit again now, so I asked him in too to meet them!"

I drew a deep breath of relief. I had played a desperate game, but I had won! I could have wished, to be sure, that my mother had not thought of bringing in Travers on that of all evenings, but I hoped that I could defy him after this.

The colonel and his people were the first to arrive, he and his wife being so effusively grateful that they made me very uncomfortable indeed; Lilian met me with downcast eyes and the faintest possible blush, but she said nothing just then. Five minutes afterward, when she and I were alone together in the conservatory, where I had brought her on pretence of showing a new begonia, she laid her hand on my sleeve and whispered, almost shyly, "Mr. Weatherhead—Algernon! Can you ever forgive me for being so cruel and unjust to you?" And I replied that, upon the whole, I could.

We were not in the conservatory long, but before we left it beautiful Lilian Roseblade had consented to make my life happy. When we reentered the drawing-room we found Frank Travers, who had been told the story of the recovery; and I observed his jaw fall as he glanced at our faces, and noted the triumphant smile which I have no doubt mine wore, and the tender, dreamy look in Lilian's soft eyes. Poor Travers! I was sorry for him, although I was not fond of him. Travers was a good type of rising young common-law barrister, tall, not bad-looking, with keen dark eyes, black whiskers, and the mobile forensic mouth which can express every shade of feeling, from deferential assent to cynical incredulity; possessed, too, of an endless flow of conversation that was decidedly agreeable, if a trifling too laboriously so, he had been a dangerous rival. But all that was over now; he saw it himself at once, and during dinner sank into dismal silence, gazing pathetically at Lilian, and sighing almost obtrusively between the courses. His stream of small talk seemed to have been cut off at the main.

"You've done a kind thing, Weatherhead," said the colonel. "I can't tell you all that dog is to me, and how I missed the poor beast. I'd quite given up all hope of ever seeing him again, and all the time there was Weatherhead, Mr. Travers, quietly searching all London till he found him! I sha'n't forget it. It shows a really kind feeling."

I saw by Travers's face that he was telling himself he would have found fifty Bingos in half the time—if he had only thought of it; he smiled a melancholy assent to all the colonel said, and then began to study me with an obviously depreciatory air.

"You can't think," I heard Mrs. Currie telling my mother, "how really touching it was to see poor Bingo's emotion at seeing all the old familiar objects again! He went up and sniffed at them all in turn, quite plainly recognising everything. And he was quite put out to find that we had moved his favourite ottoman out of the drawing-room. But he is so penitent too, and so ashamed of having run away; he kept under a chair in the hall all the morning; he wouldn't come in here, either, so we had to leave him in your garden."

"He's been sadly out of spirits all day," said Lilian; "he hasn't bitten one of the tradespeople."

"Oh, he's all right, the rascal!" said the colonel, cheerily. "He'll be after the cats again as well as ever in a day or two."

"Ah, those cats!" said my poor innocent mother. "Algy, you haven't tried the air-gun on them again lately, have you? They're worse than ever."

I troubled the colonel to pass the claret. Travers laughed for the first time. "That's a good idea," he said, in that carrying "bar-mess" voice of his; "an air-gun for cats, ha, ha! Make good bags, eh, Weatherhead?" I said that I did, very good bags, and felt I was getting painfully red in the face.

"Oh, Algy is an excellent shot—quite a sportsman," said my mother. "I remember, oh, long ago, when we lived at Hammersmith, he had a pistol, and he used to strew crumbs in the garden for the sparrows, and shoot at them out of the pantry window; he frequently hit one."

"Well," said the colonel, not much impressed by these sporting reminiscences, "don't go rolling over our Bingo by mistake, you know, Weatherhead, my boy. Not but what you've a sort of right after this—only don't. I wouldn't go through it all twice for anything."

"If you really won't take any more wine," I said, hurriedly, addressing the colonel and Travers, "suppose we all go out and have our coffee on the lawn? It—it will be cooler there." For it was getting very hot indoors, I thought.

I left Travers to amuse the ladies—he could do no more harm now; and, taking the colonel aside, I seized the opportunity, as we strolled up and down the garden path, to ask his consent to Lilian's engagement to me. He gave it cordially. "There's not a man in England," he said, "that I'd sooner see her married to after to-day. You're a quiet, steady young fellow, and you've a good kind heart. As for the money, that's neither here nor there; Lilian won't come to you without a penny, you know. But really, my boy, you can hardly believe what it is to my poor wife and me to see that dog. Why, bless my soul, look at him now! What's the matter with him, eh?"

To my unutterable horror, I saw that that miserable poodle, after begging unnoticed at the tea-table for some time, had retired to an open space before it, where he was industriously standing on his head.

We gathered round and examined the animal curiously, as he continued to balance himself gravely in his abnormal position. "Good gracious, John," cried Mrs. Currie, "I never saw Bingo do such a thing before in his life!"

"Very odd," said the colonel, putting up his glasses; "never learned that from me."

"I tell you what I fancy it is," I suggested wildly. "You see, he was always a sensitive, excitable animal, and perhaps the—the sudden joy of his return has gone to his head—upset him, you know."

They seemed disposed to accept this solution, and, indeed, I believe they would have credited Bingo with every conceivable degree of sensibility; but I felt myself that if this unhappy animal had many more of these accomplishments I was undone, for the original Bingo had never been a dog of parts.

"It's very odd," said Travers, reflectively, as the dog recovered his proper level, "but I always thought that it was half the right ear that Bingo had lost."

"So it is, isn't it?" said the colonel. "Left, eh? Well, I thought myself it was the right."

My heart almost stopped with terror; I had altogether forgotten that. I hastened to set the point at rest. "Oh, it was the left," I said, positively; "I know it because I remember so particularly thinking how odd it was that it should be the left ear, and not the right!" I told myself this should be positively my last lie.

"Why odd?" asked Frank Travers, with his most offensive Socratic manner.

"My dear fellow, I can't tell you," I said, impatiently; "everything seems odd when you come to think at all about it."

"Algernon," said Lilian, later on, "will you tell Aunt Mary and Mr. Travers and—me how it was you came to find Bingo? Mr. Travers is quite anxious to hear all about it."

I could not very well refuse; I sat down and told the story, all my own way. I painted Blagg perhaps rather bigger and blacker than life, and described an exciting scene, in which I recognised Bingo by his collar in the streets, and claimed and bore him off then and there in spite of all opposition.

I had the inexpressible pleasure of seeing Travers grinding his teeth with envy as I went on, and feeling Lilian's soft, slender hand glide silently into mine as I told my tale in the twilight.

All at once, just as I reached the climax, we heard the poodle barking furiously at the hedge which separated my garden from the road.

"There's a foreign-looking man staring over the hedge," said Lilian; "Bingo always did hate foreigners."

There certainly was a swarthy man there, and, though I had no reason for it then, somehow my heart died within me at the sight of him.

"Don't be alarmed, sir," cried the colonel; "the dog won't bite you—unless there's a hole in the hedge anywhere."

The stranger took off his small straw hat with a sweep. "Ah, I am not afraid," he said, and his accent proclaimed him a Frenchman; "he is not enrage at me. May I ask, it is pairmeet to speak viz Misterre Vezzered?"

I felt I must deal with this person alone, for I feared the worst; and, asking them to excuse me, I went to the hedge and faced the Frenchman with the frightful calm of despair. He was a short, stout little man, with blue cheeks, sparkling black eyes, and a vivacious walnut-coloured countenance; he wore a short black alpaca coat, and a large white cravat, with an immense oval malachite brooch in the centre of it, which I mention because I found myself staring mechanically at it during the interview.

"My name is Weatherhead," I began with the bearing of a detected pickpocket. "Can I be of any service to you?"

"Of a great service," he said, emphatically; "you can restore to me ze poodle vich I see zere!"

Nemesis had called at last in the shape of a rival claimant. I staggered for an instant; then I said, "Oh, I think you are under a mistake; that dog is not mine."

"I know it," he said; "zere 'as been leetle mistake, so if ze dog is not to you, you give him back to me, hein?"

"I tell you," I said, "that poodle belongs to the gentleman over there." And I pointed to the colonel, seeing that it was best now to bring him into the affair without delay.

"You are wrong," he said, doggedly; "ze poodle is my poodle! And I was direct to you—it is your name on ze carte!" And he presented me with that fatal card which I had been foolish enough to give to Blagg as a proof of my identity. I saw it all now; the old villain had betrayed me, and to earn a double reward had put the real owner on my track.

I decided to call the colonel at once, and attempt to brazen it out with the help of his sincere belief in the dog.

"Eh, what's that; what's it all about?" said the colonel, bustling up, followed at intervals by the others.

The Frenchman raised his hat again. "I do not vant to make a trouble," he began, "but zere is leetle mistake. My word of honour, sare, I see my own poodle in your garden. Ven I appeal to zis gentilman to restore 'im he reffer me to you."

"You must allow me to know my own dog, sir," said the colonel. "Why, I've had him from a pup. Bingo, old boy, you know your name, don't you?"

But the brute ignored him altogether, and began to leap wildly at the hedge in frantic efforts to join the Frenchman. It needed no Solomon to decide his ownership!

"I tell you, you 'ave got ze wrong poodle—it is my own dog, my Azor! He remember me well, you see? I lose him, it is three, four days. . . . I see a nottice zat he is found, and ven I go to ze address zey tell me,

'Oh, he is reclaim, he is gone viz a strangaire who has advertise.' Zey show me ze placard; I follow 'ere, and ven I arrive I see my poodle in ze garden before me!"

"But look here," said the colonel, impatiently; "it's all very well to say that, but how can you prove it? I give you my word that the dog belongs to me! You must prove your claim, eh, Travers?"

"Yes," said Travers, judicially; "mere assertion is no proof; it's oath against oath at present."

"Attend an instant; your poodle, was he 'ighly train, had he some talents—a dog viz tricks, eh?"

"No, he's not," said the colonel; "I don't like to see dogs taught to play the fool; there's none of that nonsense about him, sir!"

"Ah, remark him well, then. Azor, mon chou, danse donc un peu!"

And, on the foreigner's whistling a lively air, that infernal poodle rose on his hind legs and danced solemnly about half-way round the garden! We inside followed his movements with dismay.

"Why, dash it all!" cried the disgusted colonel, "he's dancing along like a d—d mountebank! But it's my Bingo, for all that!"

"You are not convince? You shall see more. Azor, ici! Pour Beesmarck, Azor!" (the poodle barked ferociously.) "Pour Gambetta!" (He wagged his tail and began to leap with joy.) "Meurs pour la patrie!" And the too accomplished animal rolled over as if killed in battle!

"Where could Bingo have picked up so much French?" cried Lilian, incredulously.

"Or so much French history?" added that serpent, Travers.

"Shall I command 'im to jump, or reverse 'imself?" inquired the obliging Frenchman.

"We've seen that, thank you," said the colonel, gloomily. "Upon my word, I don't know what to think. It can't be that that's not my Bingo after all—I'll never believe it!"

I tried a last desperate stroke. "Will you come round to the front?" I said to the Frenchman. "I'll let you in, and we can discuss the matter quietly." Then, as we walked back together, I asked him eagerly what he would take to abandon his claims and let the colonel think the poodle was his after all.

He was furious—he considered himself insulted; with great emotion he informed me that the dog was the pride of his life (it seems to be the mission of black poodles to serve as domestic comforts of this priceless kind!), that he would not part with him for twice his weight in gold.

"Figure," he began, as we joined the others, "zat zis gentilman 'ere 'as offer me money for ze dog! He agrees zat it is to me, you see? Ver' well, zen, zere is no more to be said!"

"Why, Weatherhead, have you lost faith too, then?" said the colonel.

I saw it was no good; all I wanted now was to get out of it creditably and get rid of the Frenchman. "I'm sorry to say," I replied, "that I'm afraid I've been deceived by the extraordinary likeness. I don't think, on reflection, that that is Bingo!"

"What do you think, Travers?" asked the colonel.

"Well, since you ask me," said Travers, with quite unnecessary dryness, "I never did think so."

"Nor I," said the colonel; "I thought from the first that was never my Bingo. Why, Bingo would make two of that beast!"

And Lilian and her aunt both protested that they had had their doubts from the first.

"Zen you pairmeet zat I remove 'im?" said the Frenchman.

"Certainly," said the colonel; and, after some apologies on our part for the mistake, he went off in triumph, with the detestable poodle frisking after him.

When he had gone the colonel laid his hand kindly on my shoulder. "Don't look so cut up about it, my boy," he said; "you did your best—there was a sort of likeness to any one who didn't know Bingo as we did."

Just then the Frenchman again appeared at the hedge. "A thousand pardons," he said, "but I find zis upon my dog; it is not to me. Suffer me to restore it viz many compliments."

It was Bingo's collar. Travers took it from his hand and brought it to us.

"This was on the dog when you stopped that fellow, didn't you say?" he asked me.

One more lie—and I was so weary of falsehood! "Y-yes," I said, reluctantly; "that was so."

"Very extraordinary," said Travers; "that's the wrong poodle beyond a doubt, but when he's found he's wearing the right dog's collar! Now how do you account for that?"

"My good fellow," I said, impatiently, "I'm not in the witness-box. I can't account for it. It-it's a mere coincidence!"

"But look here, my dear Weatherhead," argued Travers (whether in good faith or not I never could quite make out), "don't you see what a tremendously important link it is? Here's a dog who (as I understand the facts) had a silver collar, with his name engraved on it, round his neck at the time he was lost. Here's that identical collar turning up soon afterward round the neck of a totally different dog! We must follow this up; we must get at the bottom of it somehow! With a clue like this, we're sure to find out either the dog himself, or what's become of him! Just try to recollect exactly what happened, there's a good fellow. This is just the sort of thing I like!"

It was the sort of thing I did not enjoy at all. "You must excuse me to-night, Travers," I said, uncomfortably; "you see, just now it's rather a sore subject for me, and I'm not feeling very well!" I was grateful just then for a reassuring glance of pity and confidence from Lilian's sweet eyes, which revived my drooping spirits for the moment.

"Yes, we'll go into it to-morrow, Travers," said the colonel; "and then—hullo, why, there's that confounded Frenchman again!"

It was indeed; he came prancing back delicately, with a malicious enjoyment on his wrinkled face. "Once more I return to apologise," he said. "My poodle 'as permit 'imself ze grave indiscretion to make a very big 'ole at ze bottom of ze garden!"

I assured him that it was of no consequence. "Perhaps," he replied, looking steadily at me through his keen, half-shut eyes, "you vill not say zat ven you regard ze 'ole. And you others, I spik to you: sometimes von loses a somzing vich is qvite near all ze time. It is ver' droll, eh? my vord, ha, ha, ha!" And he ambled off, with an aggressively fiendish laugh that chilled my blood.

"What the deuce did he mean by that, eh?" said the colonel, blankly.

"Don't know," said Travers; "suppose we go and inspect the hole?"

But before that I had contrived to draw near it myself, in deadly fear lest the Frenchman's last words had contained some innuendo which I had not understood.

It was light enough still for me to see something, at the unexpected horror of which I very nearly fainted.

That thrice accursed poodle which I had been insane enough to attempt to foist upon the colonel must, it seems, have buried his supper the night before very near the spot in which I had laid Bingo, and in his attempts to exhume his bone had brought the remains of my victim to the surface!

There the corpse lay, on the very top of the excavations. Time had not, of course, improved its appearance, which was ghastly in the extreme, but still plainly recognisable by the eye of affection.

"It's a very ordinary hole," I gasped, putting myself before it and trying to turn them back. "Nothing in it—nothing at all!"

"Except one Algernon Weatherhead, Esq., eh?" whispered Travers, jocosely, in my ear.

"No; but," persisted the colonel, advancing, "look here! Has the dog damaged any of your shrubs?"

"No, no!" I cried, piteously; "quite the reverse. Let's all go indoors now; it's getting so cold!"

"See, there is a shrub or something uprooted," said the colonel, still coming nearer that fatal hole. "Why, hullo, look there! What's that?"

Lilian, who was by his side, gave a slight scream. "Uncle," she cried, "it looks like—like Bingo!"

The colonel turned suddenly upon me. "Do you hear?" he demanded, in a choked voice. "You hear what she says? Can't you speak out? Is that our Bingo?"

I gave it up at last; I only longed to be allowed to crawl away under something! "Yes," I said in a dull whisper, as I sat down heavily on a garden seat, "yes . . . that's Bingo . . . misfortune . . . shoot him . . . quite an accident!"

There was a terrible explosion after that; they saw at last how I had deceived them, and put the very worst construction upon everything. Even now I writhe impotently at times, and my cheeks smart and tingle with humiliation, as I recall that scene—the colonel's very plain speaking, Lilian's passionate reproaches and contempt, and her aunt's speechless prostration of disappointment.

I made no attempt to defend myself; I was not, perhaps, the complete villain they deemed me, but I felt dully that no doubt it all served me perfectly right.

Still I do not think I am under any obligation to put their remarks down in black and white here.

Travers had vanished at the first opportunity—whether out of delicacy, or the fear of breaking out into unseasonable mirth, I cannot say; and shortly afterward the others came to where I sat silent with bowed head, and bade me a stern and final farewell.

And then, as the last gleam of Lilian's white dress vanished down the garden path, I laid my head down on the table among the coffee-cups, and cried like a beaten child.

I got leave as soon as I could, and went abroad. The morning after my return I noticed, while shaving, that there was a small square marble tablet placed against the wall of the colonel's garden. I got my opera-glass and read—and pleasant reading it was—the following inscription:

IN AFFECTIONATE MEMORY
OF
B I N G O,
SECRETLY AND CRUELLY PUT TO DEATH,
IN COLD BLOOD,
BY A
NEIGHBOUR AND FRIEND.
JUNE, 1881.

If this explanation of mine ever reaches my neighbours' eyes, I humbly hope they will have the humanity either to take away or tone down that tablet. They cannot conceive what I suffer when curious visitors insist, as they do every day, on spelling out the words from our windows, and asking me countless questions about them!

Sometimes I meet the Curries about the village, and as they pass me with averted heads I feel myself growing crimson. Travers is almost always with Lilian now. He has given her a dog,—a fox-terrier,—and they take ostentatiously elaborate precautions to keep it out of my garden.

I should like to assure them here that they need not be under any alarm. I have shot one dog.

F. Anstey – A Concise Bibliography

Vice Versa (1882)
The Black Poodle And Other Tales (1884)
The Giant's Robe (1884)
The Tinted Venus (1885)
A Fallen Idol (1886)
Burglar Bill And Other Pieces (1888)
The Pariah (1889)
Voces Populi (1890)
Tourmalin's Time Cheques (1891)
Mr. Punch's Model Music-Hall Songs And Dramas (1892)
The Talking Horse And Other Tales (1892)
The Travelling Companions (1892)
The Man From Blankley's And Other Sketches (1893)
Mr. Punch's Pocket Ibsen (1893)
Under the Rose (1894)
Lyre and Lancet (1895)
The Statement of Stella Maberly, Written By Herself (1896)
Baboo Jabberjee, B. A. (1897)
Puppets At Large (1897)
Love Among The Lions (1898)
Paleface And Redskin (1898)
The Brass Bottle (1900)
A Bayard From Bengal (1902)
Only Toys! (1903)
Salted Almonds (1906)
Winnie, An Everyday Story (1909)
In Brief Authority (1915)
Percy and Others (1915)
The Last Load (1925)
The Would-Be Gentleman (Adapted From Molière's Le Bourgeois gentilhomme) (1927)
The Imaginary Invalid (Adapted From Molière's Le Malade imaginaire) (1929)
Humour and Fantasy (1931)
A Long Retrospect (1936)